Sight Unseen

David Carroll

Scholastic Canada Ltd.
Toronto New York London Auckland Sydney
Mexico City New Delhi Hong Kong Buenos Aires

Scholastic Canada Ltd.
604 King Street West, Toronto, Ontario M5V 1E1, Canada

Scholastic Inc.
557 Broadway, New York, NY 10012, USA

Scholastic Australia Pty Limited
PO Box 579, Gosford, NSW 2250, Australia

Scholastic New Zealand Limited
Private Bag 94407, Botany, Manukau 2163, New Zealand

Scholastic Children's Books
Euston House, 24 Eversholt Street, London NW1 1DB, UK

www.scholastic.ca

Library and Archives Canada Cataloguing in Publication

Carroll, David, 1966-, author
Sight unseen / David Carroll.

Issued in print and electronic formats.
ISBN 978-1-4431-4690-6 (pbk.).—ISBN 978-1-4431-4691-3 (ebook).—
ISBN 978-1-4431-4692-0 (Apple edition)

I. Title.

PS8605.A77724S54 2015   jC813'.6C2015-901883-8
C2015-901884-6

6 5 4 3 2 1   Printed in Canada   121   15 16 17 18 19

MIX
Paper from
responsible sources
FSC® C004071
www.fsc.org

For Kai Black

CHAPTER 1

The Scream in the Woods

None of it would've happened if not for that cougar.

Not Mislaid Lake, or the Glimmer Lines, or even hanging out with Tab. Well, Tab might have happened, since we first saw her from the dock, but we sure wouldn't've ended up at the floating island together. I'm not sure how I feel about that. On the one hand, I'm no longer a human calculator, which is good. On the other hand, I can't ride my bike or drive a car anymore. And I'm still not sure what happened to Constant.

Anyway, it was the first non-crappy day since we'd arrived at Splitsville. It was August 11th, which meant there were exactly

1,900,800 seconds left until school

and

146,806,800 seconds until Lights Out.

The panic attacks had levelled off, and Mom and Dad had brought me to the cabin to recover. I'd invited Cheese along for the ride. He was with me when I hiked up Poacher's Trail.

"Think about it," Cheese was saying. "What's so special about the Gala? There are zillions of varieties of apples in the world, but only the Gala gets to be royal. How come?"

I stepped in something soft and brown. Just mud, I hoped. "Because they taste good?" I suggested.

"Nah," said Cheese. "Granny Smiths taste way better than Galas. So does the McIntosh. It makes no sense."

He hopped over a little creek. I followed in his footsteps.

"Plus," he said, "what kind of gala is it? The Academy Awards? The VMAs?"

I didn't bother to answer. Cheese was on a roll. There was no point interrupting when he was on a roll.

"Think about it," he said. "All the other apples must be jealous. It's got to be hard on the apple community."

Poacher's Trail ran up the west side of Devil's Thumb. The path was gummier than pancake batter.

"This is brutal," said Cheese. "It's like hiking through oatmeal."

"Better than being stuck back at Splitsville," I said.

"Yes it is, brother," said Cheese. "No offence, but I've been going a bit stir-crazy back there. Seriously, I've had more fun watching my hard drive defrag."

Crap — I sank into a puddle of mud. "You're supposed to warn me about those," I said.

"Oh, right," said Cheese. "Sorry."

"Tell me what you see," I said. "Give me details."

Cheese told me about the pair of hawks circling overhead, and the little blue butterflies snacking on the wildflowers we were passing.

"You don't need to tell me absolutely *everything*," I said.

There was a noise in the woods, off to our right.

"What was that?" said Cheese.

"Rabbit," I said. "Or maybe a porcupine."

It was Mom who'd suggested I bring a friend to the cabin. "You know how squirrelly you get up there," she'd said. "And it's not like there are any other kids to hang out with."

She didn't state her real reason, of course, which was that she wanted someone who could *watch my back*. A babysitter, basically. I couldn't blame her, I guess. Not after what happened at Drag River.

She put her coffee cup down when I told her I'd invited Cheese.

"Not Spencer?" she said. "Aren't you guys getting along?"

I was too embarrassed to tell her the truth, which is that Spencer and I weren't hanging out anymore. Same for the other Skid Marks.

"I didn't know you and Cheese were close," she went on.

"We're not, really," I said. "But he's never been to the mountains. His family doesn't have much money."

That's right, Finn. You're doing him a favour. It's got nothing to do with the fact that he saved your life — right?

Cheese picked up a rock and whipped it into the woods. It cracked loudly off a tree trunk.

"I could understand if Golden Delicious apples were called royal," he continued. "They're golden, after all."

"Maybe the Queen really likes them," I said. "Or maybe they grow them in the gardens at Buckingham Palace."

"It's possible," said Cheese. "We need to find out. Put that on the list. *What's the deal with Royal Galas?*"

I pulled the Sharpie and notepad out of my pocket. We were keeping a list of *Things We Do Not Know*. Actually, I was keeping a whole bunch of lists, but Cheese and I were working on this one together. Whenever we snagged an internet connection, we'd look stuff up and educate ourselves. Then we'd scribble those things off the list. It felt good to draw a black line through the entries. Made me feel like I was getting smarter.

"Add The Hunger Games to the list," Cheese said. "Would you believe I've never seen those movies? Put down Cheesestrings, too. I don't know anything about Cheesestrings. I've never even eaten one."

I saw a flash of brown out of the corner of my eye. Some kind of bird, swooping through the forest? I didn't bother telling Cheese that I'd seen every Hunger Games movie, and that I know more about cheese strings than should be allowed. Like I said, when Cheese is on a roll, it's best to let him go.

"I want to start carrying a sword," he said.

"*Why?* For protection?" I asked.

"No, I just want to point things out really dramatically." He lunged forward, pretending to stab a tree. "Behold — a pine tree!" he cried.

And that's when we heard the scream.

It came from behind the tree Cheese was stabbing. I knew right away what it was. You don't spend ten summers in the coastal mountains without learning a thing or two about cougars.

I thought: *please no please no please no.* Cheese screamed.

I tilted my head and saw it. Huge shoulders, it looked like. Knife-blade ears, perked straight up. It swatted the ground and let out a second scream.

FYI, cougars almost never eat humans. And when they do, it's usually little ones, i.e. babies. So Cheese and I were probably safe. Then again, Cheese was pretty small.

After that, time sped up, and things happened very fast. The cougar screamed again. It sounded like a kindergarten kid getting his guts ripped out. Black dots swam in front of my eyes. Cheese took off. And then I started running after Cheese.

"Wait!" I shouted. Another scream rose up behind me — a choir of children being disembowelled.

I ran as hard as I could, praying I wouldn't trip. If I did a face plant, the cougar would sense my weakness and attack.

Don't panic, I told myself. *Just follow the trail. Just follow the brown tunnel and steer clear of the green trees on either side.*

I stumbled over some tree roots, but I kept my balance and miraculously I didn't fall. Eventually I saw Cheese's orange jersey up ahead, dancing back and forth between the trees.

"Cheese, wait up!" I shouted.

Anywhere else in the country, Devil's Thumb would be a mountain, but out here it barely counts as a pimple. Still, it's pretty high, maybe 1,200 metres, and even though we're not great runners, Cheese and I sprinted up to Halfway Rock.

"What the heck was *that*?" Cheese gasped, collapsing against the limestone outcrop.

It felt like my lungs were being squeezed by ropes. The screaming noise had faded behind us.

"Cougar," I said.

"Did you see it?"

"Yeah," I said. "Didn't you?"

Cheese shook his head and sucked in air.

"It was probably a female," I said. "Protecting her kittens."

Cheese took off his glasses and rubbed his forehead. Then

he put them back on and looked behind us. "Do you think it's stalking us?"

"Doubt it," I said.

Cheese stood back up. "Did you hear that thing scream? That was a *wail of death*."

We laughed, and it felt good to laugh. We both kept glancing down the trail.

"Add that to the list of stuff we know," Cheese said. "Cougars scream like banshees."

I pulled out the notepad and wrote it down.

"You're sure it was a cougar?" he said.

"Of course," I said.

"Yeah, but how can you tell? I mean, with your vision . . . It might've just been a bobcat or something."

I shrugged and drank from my water bottle.

"Sorry," he said. "But I have to ask."

I capped the bottle and slipped it back into my knapsack. "It wasn't a bobcat," I said. "And we should probably dump the rest of our food, just in case it follows the scent."

We went through the knapsack and wolfed down the sandwiches. Mom had packed some granola bars, so we unwrapped them and ate those, too.

"Humans aren't their natural prey," I said. "More people get killed by moose than by cougars."

Cheese stared at me. Then he said, "You know your nostrils flare open really wide when you talk, right? They're like circus tents or something. I can practically see your brain."

Cheese could be pretty tactless sometimes. He's one of the *gifted* kids at school, which means . . . well, you know what it means.

"So?" I said. "What am I supposed to do about it?"

"Nothing," said Cheese. "I'm just pointing it out. In case you somehow missed it in the mirror."

I pulled at my eyebrows, and a few hairs popped loose. I could feel my heartbeat speeding up. "Don't be such a greasebag," I said.

"You're the greasebag," said Cheese. "Hey, how far did we just come?"

"From the cougar den?" I said. "Nine hundred and fifty steps. So probably a kilometre or so."

Cheese sighed. "How do we get back to Splitsville from here?"

"There's another trail," I said. "On the other side of the Thumb. But we have to climb to the summit to reach it."

We pressed on. The sun was warm, but now and again we crossed small streams, and we'd pass through these little waves of cool air. Cheese walked ahead, and when we came to a narrow section of trail, I could hear loose stones popping under his shoes and rolling over the edge of the cliff.

Finally we came over the summit. The trail levelled out and we were on a flat plateau.

"At last," said Cheese. "Hey, nice view."

I sat down on a boulder and looked around. People always rave about the scenery in the Rockies, but the mountains look more like steamed spinach to me. The highest peak, the Mazinaw, was a plum-coloured bruise off to the east.

"What's that?" I said.

"Where?" said Cheese.

"Down in that star-shaped lake."

I turned sideways to get a better view. Most of the lakes

were long and narrow, except for one that looked like a star-fish.

"Down there," I said. "It's flashing, and it's blue."

Cheese looked down. "I can see an island," he said. "But I don't see anything blue. Aside from the water, I mean."

It blinked like a strobe light. It was blue, like the flame of a blowtorch.

Cheese held up his phone. He was taking a video.

"Can you see the flickering?" I asked.

"No," he said. "But there's a weird little island. And it's *moving*." He stared at his phone and then back down at the valley.

"Islands don't move," I said.

"Of this, I am aware," said Cheese.

He shielded the screen from the sunlight and stared at it. Then he swiped to make the image larger, and passed the phone to me.

I held the screen right up to my face. The image was small and grainy, but it looked like an island, all right. "You seriously think this thing is moving?" I said.

Cheese swung his head and looked down at the lake. "It's not setting any speed records," he said. "But it is moving."

I looked down at the lake and saw the flashing blue light. Then I looked back at the phone. Nothing was flashing on the screen. "Maybe it's a hunting blind," I said. "Or a barge that someone dressed up to look like an island."

"It isn't any barge," said Cheese. "But it's still moving. It's actually got a tiny wake."

I handed the phone back to Cheese.

"There has to be a logical explanation," I said. "Islands just don't move like that."

"Not unless they float," Cheese said. He glanced behind us, down the trail.

"Right," I said. "We'd better get going. There's a big cat down there somewhere."

And for better or worse, and there was an awful lot of worse, the summer got a lot less boring after that.

CHAPTER 2

The Floating Island

1,872,000 seconds left until school
140,778,000 seconds until Lights Out

On the bright side, the island took our minds off the cougar.

"Who ever heard of an island that floats?" Cheese said. "Put that on the list. At the *top* of the list."

"I still like the hunting-blind theory," I said.

"But there were trees," said Cheese. "They were, like, five metres tall."

He checked his phone, but he didn't have any reception. "I thought there was a cell tower out here somewhere," he said.

"There is," I said. "But it's at the far end of Bully Bay, past those hills. You might get something when we're closer to the lake."

"Hang on," Cheese said suddenly. "I just got service — well, one bar anyway." He did a quick search for *floating island*.

"Get any hits?" I asked.

"Uh, zillions," he said.

"No *way*," I said.

Cheese cleared his throat and began to read: "A floating island, prepared according to the traditional French recipe, is a gastronomic delight. Mouth-watering clouds of softly poached meringue, floating in a lagoon of vanilla custard . . . "

"A floating island is a dessert?" I said.

"Not just any dessert. You should see the picture. It looks like a marshmallow mountain with lava custard pouring down the sides."

"Next," I said.

He swiped the screen, read silently for a moment, and then said, "Cool!"

"What?"

He looked up at me. "Islands really can float."

"Seriously?"

He nodded. "It doesn't start out as an island," he said. "At first it's just a point of land until a storm rips it off the shore. With the right kind of soil and plants — peat and cattails and stuff — it can be buoyant enough to float."

"That really happens?" I asked. "Even when there are *trees* on it?"

Cheese nodded. "It's rare, but it definitely happens," he said. "Maybe they have to be small trees. There are pictures if you want to see."

I looked at the screen. "That's crazy," I said.

"I know," Cheese said. "Total mindfreak."

He looked down at his phone. "It's also known as a floaton."

"Ew," I said. "Sounds like something you'd find in a toilet."

"Thank you for that visual."

Cheese shoved his phone back into his pocket and we continued walking down the trail. My mind was whirring like a salad spinner.

"How long do these islands float around?" I asked Cheese.

11

"Not that long," he said. "They migrate around the lake, blown by the wind. Usually a thunderstorm tears them to pieces."

The trail followed the bank of a small creek, which tumbled over little waterfalls every hundred metres or so. Eventually we could see Nanavisik Lake through the trees. We ran down to the shoreline. Cheese knelt down and kissed the rocks.

"And you thought this trip would be boring," I said.

"It was looking grim, you have to admit," said Cheese.

We rolled up our pants and waded into the lake, then walked along the pebble beach to Splitsville. "Hey," I said. "Don't mention the cougar to my parents."

"Why not?"

"Because they'll never let us outside ever again."

A word about Splitsville, my family's freaky cabin. It's perched on the edge of a cliff, on these crazy long stilts. Every year there's some kind of disaster. One year the roof collapsed; another time a bear moved in and hibernated in the kitchen all winter. When the compostable toilet exploded, my mom lost it.

"That's it," she shouted at my dad. "I'm outta here; I'm *splitsville!*"

The name stuck. It's been Splitsville ever since.

Mom was standing on the deck when we arrived. "There you are!" she shouted down. "That took longer than expected."

We finally got to the top of the stairs. Mom was drinking tea from her neon yellow mug. The one that says *Thou Shalt Not Speak Until I Finish This Coffee.*

"Couldn't be bothered to change into your bathing suits?" she asked, staring at our wet jeans.

I shrugged. Cheese flopped into the hammock.

"See anything interesting?" Mom asked.

No nothing much. Just a floating island and a cougar.

"We sure did," said Cheese, making my heart stop. But then he said, "I found your manzanita bushes. Hang on."

He pulled his phone out of his pocket and rolled out of the hammock. He'd taken pictures for my mom. The guy was good.

"They're gorgeous," said Mom, scrolling through the shots. "Look, that one has produced berries already!"

You'd think he'd taken pictures of the Eiffel Tower.

"I'd love to print these out," Mom said. "They'd make a great subject for a painting."

"I'll text them to you," Cheese said.

"Could you email them instead?" Mom said. "I don't text."

"Sure, no problem."

Cheese sat back down on the hammock. Mom emptied the dregs of her tea over the railing. I heard the splash against the forest floor a second later. "Hey, Mom," I said, "have you ever heard of a *floaton*?"

I decided to throw it out there, just in case. Mom leaned back against the sliding screen door. "What's a floaton?" she said.

"We think it's an island that floats," I said.

She stared at the puddle that was forming beneath my dripping pants. "I'm not the one to ask," she said. "Your father would probably know all about it, though." She opened the screen door and went inside.

"Is he coming home tonight?" I asked.

"Who knows?" She was opening and closing kitchen cupboards now. "We're having kale salad for dinner. Is that okay with you, Cheese?"

"I *love* kale salad!" Cheese said.

A colossal lie. Give him credit, though. The guy knew how to sell it.

"Plus yam chops," Mom added. "And I could poach you boys an egg. We have country-fresh eggs, if you like."

"I do love a good country-fresh egg," Cheese said. "But yam chops and kale should be enough."

I soft-punched Cheese's shoulder. He could make me laugh sometimes.

"Hang on," he said. "I snagged a connection."

He tapped the screen with his thumbs.

"Whatcha doing?" I asked.

"Looking at maps," he said. "Trying to find that island."

Mom was pacing back and forth in the kitchen. "Hey, Johnston," she said suddenly. "Caught our dinner yet?"

Johnston was my dad. So he'd answered his phone.

"You coming home tonight or what?" Mom said. "I've got two mouths to feed and they're getting — "

"Ask him about the floaton!" I called out.

"Hang on, the boys have a question," Mom said. "Have you ever heard of a floaton? The boys think it's some kind of floating island."

I walked over to the screen door. I slid it open and shut. Once, twice, three times.

"Honey, don't do that," Mom said. "You're letting in mosquitoes."

I opened and shut it one more time, then I latched the door and sat down on the edge of the hammock. My brain was racing like a hummingbird's wings. *Just 23,400 seconds left in the day,* I thought, *and 1,866,600 left in the summer . . .*

"I wouldn't know," Mom said to the phone. "You'll have to ask them. Come back and have supper with us if you — "

Another long pause. Mom sighed.

"Okay, fine. You tell them that when you come back."

She set the phone down on the counter. I looked at her through the window.

"Is he coming home?" I asked.

"Probably not tonight," she said, taking a sip from her mug.

"Had he heard of a floaton?" Cheese asked.

"Yeah, except he called it a tussock." Mom set her mug in the sink and turned on the tap. "He didn't think it was an island, exactly. More like a floating mass of vegetation. He wanted to know if you boys had seen one."

"We didn't," Cheese said, a little too quickly. "We just came across the word, and we were curious."

Mom squashed a bug against the screen and then walked over to the fridge.

"Why did Dad want to know if we'd seen one?" I asked.

"Oh, you know your father. If it has anything to do with fishing, he wants to know all about it."

She came back to the sink with a head of lettuce and ran it under the tap. Then she crammed it into the salad spinner.

"What does a floaton have to do with fishing?" Cheese asked.

Mom dried her hands. "Something to do with feeder fish," she said. "The minnows hang out underneath, nibbling the algae. That attracts larger fish, which attracts crazy people like Finn's father."

* * *

After dinner we went down to the lake. Cheese went first, running fast. I followed after, counting the steps as I went. There are 272, not counting the ramp at the bottom. I know which ones are loose (21 and 182) and which one is home to a family of chipmunks (103).

Cheese was playing with his phone when I got down to the dock.

"Find the island?" I asked.

He shook his head. "But those images are probably a few years old. The floating island probably didn't exist back then, not if they tend to break up easily."

He shoved his phone into his pocket and tossed a pebble into the water. I heard it splash.

"It's still pretty weird," I said. "We should go back there and take another look."

"Without getting eaten by the cougar," Cheese said.

"That does add a bit of spice," I agreed.

A yellow laser beam was zapping my eyeballs. It was coming from the far end of the lake.

"Whoa," I said. "Is that light from the mountain?"

Cheese shielded his eyes. "Yeah. The sun's reflecting off the peak. There must be quartz on the summit."

"It's the big one?" I asked.

"Yep. The Mastodon, you called it."

"The Mazinaw."

"Right."

I walked out to the end of the dock, shielding my eyes. The gap in the clouds slid shut, extinguishing the sun. I peeled off my T-shirt and jumped into the lake. The water

16

was icy, but it felt good and I stayed in for a few minutes.

"If we wanted to check out that lake," Cheese asked, "would we have to take the same trail we took today?"

I swam a few metres out from the dock and treaded water. "I guess we could canoe across our lake and hike through the forest," I said. "It'd be gnarly, since there isn't a trail, but at least we wouldn't have to pass that cougar."

Cheese splashed his hand in the lake. "Think your dad would let you use the motorboat?" he asked.

"Not in a million years."

A fish came up and grabbed a bug off the surface of the lake right beside me. It must've been a big one, since it made a loud splash. I swam to the ladder, pulled myself onto the dock and wrapped my towel around me.

"You know how to paddle a canoe, right?" I asked Cheese.

"Sorta," he said.

Something swooped low over the water, darting past my right ear. A bat? Probably. The lake glowed like a blue lamp.

"We could paddle to Bully Bay in forty-five minutes or less," I said. "Then we could try hiking up through the woods."

I squeezed the water out of the corners of my eyes. The mountains looked like they'd been smudged with charcoal.

Suddenly I heard a soft, liquid sound.

"Hey," Cheese whispered. "We've got company."

"Where?" I asked.

Cheese pointed into the twilight.

I couldn't see much of anything. "Who is it?" I asked.

"Dunno," Cheese whispered. "Some kind of boat."

The gurgling was getting closer: 15 metres . . . 10 metres . . . 5.

Suddenly I saw a spear of colour. A neon yellow kayak

was slicing through the water like a knife.

Cheese raised his hand. *"Bonne soirée, madame,"* he said.

Silence. The kayak slid past the edge of the dock. A girl's voice drifted over the water. *"Boa noite, amigo."*

Another paddle stroke and the kayak vanished into the murk. The black line of its wake curled under the dock.

"A girl," Cheese said.

"Yeah, I kinda figured."

Out on the water, I heard a snicker. I pulled my T-shirt over my head and slung my towel around my neck.

The sky was now a deep plum colour. The sound of the kayak paddle faded away.

"Bonne soirée?" I said.

"I wanted to be memorable," said Cheese.

I snorted.

Cheese slapped at a mosquito on his knee. "We all have to use our gifts," he said. "Not everyone has the perfect shoulder-to-waist ratio like you."

Perfect shoulder-to-waist ratio? Where'd that come from?

"You called her *madame*," I pointed out.

"That's right," said Cheese.

"You know *madame* means married woman, right?"

Silence from Cheese. "Seriously?" he said.

"Duh. You should've said *mademoiselle*. Actually, no. You should've said *señorita*. She was speaking Spanish, not French."

Cheese said nothing.

I felt around for my sneakers. Had I worn them to the dock? I couldn't remember.

"Did you see her face?" I asked.

"Does it matter?" said Cheese.

"Of course it matters," I said. "I want to know if she was cute."

"Depends."

"On what?"

"On what you mean by cute."

Just humour me, I thought. *Throw me a bone.* "Did she have a horsey face?" I said.

Cheese threw another rock at the lake, and I heard it skip six or seven times. "She had an oval face with well-structured features," he said. "A slightly turned-up nose, which isn't an impediment."

I found my sneakers and pulled them on. "What about her hair?" I asked.

"Sand-coloured," said Cheese. "Same colour as Minnow's."

Great. Just great. He'd dropped the M bomb. He knew what he was doing, too. My mind started spinning.

"I think I see a planet," Cheese said, staring up at the sky. "Gotta be Venus. Too bright to be anything else."

I didn't answer. I can't see stars properly anymore. Some nights the sky looks gluey, but that's about it.

I checked my phone, but there wasn't anything new. Not from Minnow, and not from any of the Skid Marks. I sat back down on the dock and leaned back on my elbows. Then I stood up again and paced up and down the ramp.

"Oh, wow," said Cheese. "I think I can see Jupiter now, too. This is amazing. Summer is definitely looking up."

Like I said, Cheese is gifted at being annoying. I walked up the ramp, holding the railing, counting the steps as I went.

CHAPTER
3

The Grenade

The grenade exploded one day after my thirteenth birthday. I remember because that's the day I started counting.

Speaking of which, here's your latest update: I had 1,854,000 seconds left until the end of summer. School started on Tuesday, September 2nd, at 8 a.m. That was zero hour for me. The end of my freedom.

And then there was that bigger number.

The number at the top of the *List of Things I Know*.

Formula for Determining the Lights-Out Number:

1629 days to Lights Out

x 24 hours in a day

+ 4 additional hours

x 60 minutes in an hour

x 60 seconds in a minute

= 140,760,000 seconds until Lights Out

"That's just the doctor's estimate," Mom had said. "You might have a lot more time than that."

"I might have less time, too," I said.

"Fine," said Mom. "Be a pessimist."

It was last January. My fourth eye appointment in three weeks. And it wasn't with my ordinary optometrist this time. It was with an ophthalmologist named Dr. Zhang. Both my parents came along, which was suspicious. Dad never came to those things.

After 90 minutes of eye drops and flashing lights, Dr. Zhang led me into a small, yellow room. "Wait here while I speak with your parents," she said.

"They're my eyes," I said. "Don't I get to hear?"

Dr. Zhang looked like a blob of white. I think she was smiling, but, thanks to those nasty eye drops, it was hard to tell. "You and I will have a follow-up meeting next week," she said. "But right now, I need to speak with your parents alone."

An hour later, in the car driving home, I still didn't have a clue what was going on. Mom and Dad were in the front seat, saying zilch. A Michael Jackson song was playing on the radio.

"I need glasses, don't I?" I said.

I already knew that my vision was messed up. Like, I couldn't remember the last time I'd scored a goal in ball hockey. My friends had been calling me *Blindfold Johnston* for months, because I'd only scored three goals all year, and they were lucky ones.

"No," Mom said, "you don't need glasses."

"Seriously?" I could barely believe it. "That's great!"

Mom and Dad glanced at each other. Then Dad pulled the car over to the side of the road. That's the moment I remember best. Dad — who never stopped for anything —

pulling the car onto the gravel shoulder.

"What's wrong?" I asked. My stomach was suddenly in ropes.

Dad turned around and reached one arm over the seat. His eyes were red, as though he'd been crying. "I'm sorry I didn't believe you," he said. "When you crashed your bike into the river. I should've listened. I should have been . . . "

I couldn't take my eyes off his face. In thirteen years I'd never seen him cry. Mom was watching me through the sun visor mirror. Her face was as flat as a frozen pond.

"It just didn't add up, the way you explained it," Dad said. "How could anyone ride off a *cliff*? I just assumed . . . God, I'm sorry."

Michael Jackson was singing about being really, really bad. Mom snapped the radio off. The car made ticking sounds as the engine cooled.

"But what did Dr. Zhang say?" I asked.

Mom sighed and stared out the passenger window and I could tell that she wanted to light up a smoke. She reached for a Kleenex. Her winter coat crackled.

Suddenly Dad reached out. He tried to take my hand. I snapped my fist back, and his arm just hung there over the seat.

"Finn," he said, "I'm so, so sorry."

And that was how I found out I was going blind.

CHAPTER
4

Scrambled Eyeballs

You don't want to know about my stupid disease.

Believe me: YOU DON'T WANNA KNOW.

It's beyond boring. And totally depressing. And I am approximately five hundred per cent done with telling people about it.

Believe it or not, when I was first diagnosed, I thought it would make me a total chick magnet. I kept thinking about all those awesome blind musicians — Stevie Wonder and Ray Charles and Jeff Healey and . . . well . . .

Okay, so maybe there aren't so many. Still. I figured the girls at my school would feel sorry for me and want to take care of me and stuff. Boy, did I get that one wrong.

Attention passengers. We have a situation. Please make your way to the nearest emergency exit . . .

Slowly but surely, the Skid Marks all unfollowed me on Strava, which totally sucked, since it's basically Facebook for cyclists, and I spend half my life on the thing.

Suddenly I wasn't getting any comments or kudos, which I guess wasn't surprising, considering I hadn't uploaded a new ride in, like, forever. But then my friends started avoiding me in the hallway at school, too, and sat at the far end of the caf. Finally even Minnow stopped hanging out by my locker. My disease didn't make me a chick magnet. It made me the opposite. Chick repellant.

It's called Stargardt disease, by the way. It's basically Kryptonite to your eyeballs.

"The retina is like a movie screen at the back of your eyeball," Dr. Zhang explained. "It's where all the images get projected. Unfortunately, the disease is causing scarring. It looks a bit like scrambled eggs back there."

Dr. Zhang showed me a picture of my eyeballs. You could see the veins and blood vessels and everything. There was all this yellow junk swirling around. That was the disease, firing paintballs at my retinas.

"So what's the cure?" I asked.

"I'm afraid there isn't one," Dr. Zhang said. "Not yet. But there are some promising experimental treatments. They've done stem cell therapy with rats, and it's been very successful. Possibly in twenty years we'll have a human treatment."

I'm sorry — did you say TWENTY YEARS?

"Hope for the best but plan for the worst," Dr. Zhang said. "That's what I always tell my patients."

"How long until I'm totally blind?" I asked.

Dr. Zhang sat down on a chair across from me. "You'll never be a hundred per cent blind," she said. "You'll always see some light and shapes. And your peripheral vision should remain pretty much intact. That's your side vision. The disease doesn't affect that at all."

I stared at the floor, saying nothing.

"I know it sounds bad," she said, "but peripheral vision

is actually pretty important. It helps you move around safely and avoid obstacles."

"How much of my eyesight will I get to keep?" I said.

"Hard to say," Dr. Zhang said. "Maybe ten per cent. Which means you'll be legally blind."

It felt like all the air had gone out of the room.

"But you'll still have some independence," she went on. "You might not even need a cane."

"How long?" I asked. "How long until . . . *lights out*?"

Dr. Zhang leaned forward and rested her elbows on her knees. She was staring right at me, but I couldn't bring myself to meet her eyes. "Every case is different, and stress can make things worse," she said. "But in general terms, I'd say you've got five years, give or take."

I looked at the chart of letters on the wall. I could read the big *E* at the top, and most of the second row, but then the third row was super fuzzy and I couldn't read anything at all below that.

"Seriously?" I said. "Five years?"

"It could be longer," said Dr. Zhang. "As I said, every case is different."

When she said that, I felt like I was going to puke.

"Things will be challenging for a while," Dr. Zhang said. "Some of your hobbies will probably have to change."

Probably have to change? Who was she kidding?

I'd already had to quit mountain biking.

I was useless at ball hockey.

Even the Xbox was giving me headaches.

"It's not an easy transition, I know," said Dr. Zhang. "But you'll find new passions to take their place. In time."

TV shows — out.

Movies — out.

Basketball — don't make me laugh.

Playing guitar — who even knew?

Basically, my days of having fun were over.

Now, I had a little over two weeks left in the summer. I had to make it count.

CHAPTER
5

Going, Going, Gone

Seconds left until school: 1,832,400
Until Lights Out: 140,738,400

I couldn't get to sleep that night. No surprise there: I'd barely slept in months. I'd become a pretty good insomniac since getting that bad news about my eyes, so most nights I listened to music or tried playing games online. Of course, I couldn't get any Wi-Fi at Splitsville, so I just lay on my bed, thinking of things to add to the list of *Things We Do Not Know*.

The list was getting long. Yes, I always wrote with a Sharpie, so my printing was larger than most people's; but still, the list took up twelve pages of my spiral notebook!

I took a stack of yellow sticky notes and stuck them in a column on the wall. Then I wrote a different phrase on each of the notes.

What's with Royal Galas?

Asparagus pee.

Why do ninjas run with their arms behind their backs?

The column of notes went from the floor to way above my head.

Then I did the same thing with the list of *Things We*

Know. That list only came up to my waist.

Across the hallway, I could hear Cheese flopping around on his bed. It was 3:17 a.m. I wasn't the slightest bit tired.

I tried writing down some more things I knew.

Minnow hates my guts.

Spencer hates my guts.

My parents think I'm useless.

I sighed and crumpled the notes up. That was just personal crap, not worth sticking on the wall. The list was intended for things that mattered. I wrote *Stargardt disease*, and stuck that on the wall. Yeah, I knew that one pretty good.

Eventually I slept. When I woke up, the sun was blasting through my window like a death ray, and my eyes felt like they were coated in sand. I blinked a few times and it was like FRAAAAAAA! So I squirted in some drops, but they didn't help much. I swallowed an Aspirin and put on my sunglasses and went down to the dock, counting the steps. The sunshine was pouring through a gap in the mountains and the Mazinaw was bright pink. Mist was rising off the lake. I jumped into the water and screamed from the cold. Then I climbed out and lay down on the dock.

Slowly but surely, the sun warmed me up. My eyes felt a little bit better.

1,814,400 seconds left in the summer.

Now 1,814,399.

Now 1,814,398.

A white blob moved at the far end of the lake. A sailboat? A seaplane? A cloud of radioactive steam?

I had no idea what it was, of course.

I grabbed my phone and tapped the chat icon. There was

a green dot beside Minnow's name, so I sent her a message.

Hey you, I typed. SEND.

No response.

What's happening? SEND.

Nothing.

I held up the phone and took a picture of the lake. I had no idea if it was blurry, but I attached the jpeg anyway.

Remember this? I typed. SEND.

I waited for my phone to vibrate, but nothing happened. The green circle beside Minnow's name blinked out. She'd logged off.

I heard a noise. Cheese, clomping down the steps. "Yo, Finn," he shouted down.

"Hey," I replied.

He clomped his way onto the dock. Sounded like he was wearing wooden clogs or something. "Check this out," he said. "I found it on the bookshelf."

He sat down beside me and unfolded a big sheet of paper. A map. He turned it sideways so I could see.

"It's more detailed than what I found online," he said. "It doesn't show the island either, of course."

He placed his finger in the middle of the map. I leaned forward and saw the star-shaped lake. It was surrounded by dark green: heavy forest. Populated with grizzly bears and cougars, most likely.

"It'll be a tough hike," I said. "But I bet we can do it. Do you have a GPS app on your phone?"

"Of course," Cheese said. "But we should take a compass, too."

"No problem," I said. My dad had one upstairs.

"Good," Cheese said. "And look at this." He shifted his finger a couple of centimetres.

I leaned down and saw a tiny blue squiggle. "What's that?" I asked.

"A river," Cheese said. "It cuts through the forest and goes straight to that lake. If we can find that river, then it'll lead us to the lake."

I stared at the blue line. It meandered aimlessly for a kilometre or more, and then it connected with one of the arms of the star-shaped lake.

"We need to find that river," I said.

"We will," said Cheese, folding up the map. "But we should start soon, if we're going today."

I went upstairs and filled a knapsack with some fruit and some granola bars. Mom was still asleep, so I wrote her a note. Then I grabbed two life jackets and the compass and went back down to the lake.

Cheese had grabbed two paddles from the dock box and had flipped the canoe over and slid it into the water.

"Your mom doesn't mind you taking off?" he asked.

"She won't wake up for a while," I said. "Besides, I left her a note."

Cheese was doing something with a plastic bag.

"What are you doing?" I asked.

"Putting the map in a Ziploc bag, see?"

"How come?"

"In case we tip," he said, slipping his phone into the bag along with the map.

"We won't tip. I've been coming up here for years, and I've never tipped."

Cheese shrugged and pulled on a life jacket that was way too big, and then jumped into the canoe as if it was a regular boat.

"Easy," I said. "Hold the gunwales for balance."

"Oh, right. Sorry." His voice sounded shaky. "It's been a while since I canoed."

I turned to the side so I could see his face better. It was red and he was holding tightly to the thwart. *Bet he's never even been in a canoe before.*

I stepped in behind him, holding the gunwales. "Kneel down," I said.

"Be serious," he said.

"I am serious," I said. "It makes the canoe more stable."

"But it hurts my knees."

I grabbed my towel off the dock and tossed it forward. "Kneel on that," I said.

Cheese folded the towel and wedged it under his knees while I pulled my life jacket over my shoulders. Then I pressed the blade of my paddle against the end of the dock and pushed off. Cheese picked up his paddle, too, but he didn't have a clue what he was doing. He kept clunking it against the hull of the canoe.

"Which side should I row on?" he asked.

"Doesn't matter," I said. "You paddle left, and I'll paddle right. If you get tired, let me know, and we'll trade."

The canoe zigzagged badly at first, but I soon got used to Cheese's paddling and managed to keep the boat on a fairly straight course.

"Aim for that cellphone tower," said Cheese. "If it's the same one that's on the map, then it's right where we want to go."

"I can't see any tower," I said. "Just tell me whether I need to steer right or left."

"Seriously?" said Cheese. "You can't see that tower?"

"It's hard to see much of anything when the sun is this bright," I said.

We paddled through a narrow channel. Rickety wooden docks stuck out from the shoreline, and wooden steps led up to other cabins in the cliffs.

Cheese looked over the side of the canoe. "It's really deep here," he called back.

I stopped paddling. Cheese leaned out of the canoe.

"Careful," I said.

"Relax," he said. His bangs were touching the water.

I couldn't help myself. I lurched to one side. The canoe tilted violently.

"Hey!" Cheese shrieked.

His head went under and his paddle clacked against the thwart. I shifted my weight to steady the canoe.

Cheese glared back at me, hair dripping. "What was that?"

I couldn't stop laughing. Seriously. Couldn't stop.

"You greasebag. You know I don't swim."

"What can I say? The seas got angry."

Cheese used my towel to dry his hair.

"Oh, come on," I said. "I earned the Bronze Star. I'd pull you back in if you went overboard."

"And what about my phone?" Cheese said. "Have you got two hundred dollars to buy me a new one if it gets soaked?"

"You put it in the Ziploc bag, remember?"

Cheese glared at me and then, without any warning, picked up his paddle and chucked it into the lake.

"Oh, now *that's* mature," I said.

"Do your own paddling from now on," Cheese said.

I dipped my hat into the water and wrung it out and pressed it down on my head so that the cool water trickled down the back of my neck. Then I turned the canoe around and steered us back toward the missing paddle. "Okay," I said. "Where is it?"

Cheese stared straight ahead. "Promise not to do that again."

A gust of wind blew us sideways. "All right," I said. "I promise."

Cheese pointed, and I turned the canoe to starboard. He reached over the gunwale and grabbed his paddle. For some time after that, there was silence between us.

"I'm sorry," I said. "I seriously couldn't help it."

"That's because you're lame," said Cheese. "Put that on the list. Finn's supremely lame."

Warm air floated across the lake; it smelled like sand. I wished I hadn't scared Cheese like that. He was right; I could be a real bonehead sometimes.

Eventually he spoke. "I just had a winning idea," he said.

"Oh, really?" I said. Cheese was always having *winning ideas*.

"You know how pizzas are round or square?" Cheese said. "We should open a restaurant where the pizzas are *triangular*."

I let out a blast of laughter.

"Seriously," said Cheese, "it's never been done, I don't think. All the toppings could be triangular too. Pineapple, mushrooms, pepperoni."

"I can see triangular pineapple," I said, "but what about olives? They're round."

"That'll be harder," Cheese said, his life jacket bunching up around his ears. "We'll hire a research and development team. They'll have to figure it out."

A pair of seagulls was squawking above us. We must've been too close to their nest. Any moment they'd start dive-bombing the canoe.

"We should start a company together," Cheese said. "This concept is worth millions. More."

I laughed. Canoeing wasn't as fun as biking, but it felt good to sweat and to be working my muscles.

"We'll only run the business until it becomes successful," Cheese said. "And then we'll sell it for a billion dollars."

Suddenly it hit me that I hadn't done any counting. I hadn't counted the seconds, or my paddle strokes, or anything. The last time I'd counted had been . . . back when I texted Minnow. That had to be an hour ago, at least.

"I just forgot about my eyes," I muttered.

"What?" said Cheese.

"I forgot I'm going blind," I said. "Just for a second. Then I remembered again. But for a second there, I totally forgot."

Cheese put down his paddle. "Do you worry about your eyes all the time?"

"Pretty much," I said.

"That sucks," said Cheese.

A motorboat buzzed past us, pulling one or maybe two water skiers. They swooped from side to side, carving huge arcs of spray out of the lake.

"I'm serious about this business idea," Cheese said. "And

I think it's a good plan for you. You want to be running your own company, Finn. That way, nobody can ever fire you. People with disabilities have a hard time finding and keeping jobs. You know that, right?"

And just like that, he'd ruined the moment. Like I said, the guy's gifted. He's got a gift for being annoying.

"What's wrong?" said Cheese.

"Just forget it," I said.

"Seriously," he said, "you'd make an amazing business partner. I'm trusting you to keep this idea secret. It's worth millions if we do it right. More."

I was done with this conversation. Totally done. I dipped my paddle into the lake. I wanted to go back to 5 minutes ago, to that moment when I forgot about my eyes.

I couldn't remember that ever happening before. I was always spinning out about one thing or another — like what if I had to eventually get a white cane. Or what if I got smacked by a car while crossing a parking lot.

"We need to go farther right," said Cheese. "That's better. Cell tower's dead ahead."

I adjusted our course, and we paddled toward the shore. The land drew in on both sides of us, and after a couple of minutes, we crunched onto a pebble beach.

"Perfect," said Cheese, climbing out and tying the bowline to a floating log. "We'll just climb up the ridge to the tower. Once we find it, we should be able to see the river, no problem."

We took off our life jackets and climbed up the embankment. There wasn't any trail, so we pushed through the forest.

Suddenly the ground dropped away.

"Whoa!" I yelped.

"You okay?" said Cheese.

"You bet," I said. "But you need to warn me when we're going downhill." I stood back up and brushed off my hands and knees.

"You couldn't see that dip?" Cheese asked.

I didn't say anything.

Cheese stared at me. Then he shook his head. "Sorry, Finn, I just keep forgetting about your eyes. You fake it so well, you know? So keep reminding me, okay?"

From that point on, Cheese stayed just a step or two ahead of me on the trail. I felt like a jerk for scaring him in the canoe. We climbed uphill for a few more minutes. Finally we broke out of the trees and came into a meadow. I pulled my sunglasses over my eyes.

"Here's the tower," Cheese said.

It climbed straight into the sky. A little metal shed huddled at its base. A fence ran around the shed and tall weeds grew up around the fence.

"Can you see the river from up here?" I asked.

Cheese looked around. "No."

Grasshoppers were whizzing through the air. I couldn't be sure, but I thought Cheese was wearing a *My Little Pony* T-shirt.

"Okay, so what's the plan?" I asked. "If we keep heading south, we'll eventually hit the river, right?"

"Yeah, but we'll have to bushwhack through more forest. It's another kilometre at least. You up for that?"

We pushed on. The meadow was filled with wildflowers, and smelled like one of those expensive soap stores. Bright yellow blobs of sun sparkled on the ground, making it hard for me to see the shadows. Luckily, Cheese stayed closer to me than ever, barking out the trail conditions with every step. "Fifteen-centimetre drop here . . . Tree branches coming your way in three . . . two . . . one."

Neither of us mentioned the cougar, although I was sure Cheese was thinking about it as much as me. I distracted myself with other thoughts, like, what would we do if we actually found the lake? How would we get to the island without a boat? We should've brought an air mattress along.

"Shhhh," said Cheese.

"What?" I said.

"I heard something."

Please no please no please no.

We stood still and listened. I heard something, too, but not an animal. "It sounds like a bike bell," I said.

"No," said Cheese. "It's running water. It must be our river. Come on!"

We pushed through more forest, tree branches scraping against our faces, and then there it was — a sparkling stream. Cheese and I clattered down the gravel embankment. We waded right in and I cupped my hands and took a sip.

"Think it's safe to drink?" Cheese asked.

"Of course," I said. "It comes from glaciers." The water was icy and clear. It tasted gravelly but good.

For the next 20 minutes, we walked upstream. The farther we walked, the narrower the stream got. Soon it became so small we could step across it. A few minutes later it disappeared altogether.

"Where'd it go?" said Cheese.

"Underground."

We could hear the water gurgling beneath our feet.

"The lake can't be far," said Cheese. "I bet we could see it, if it weren't for all these trees."

I looked around. Every direction looked the same. A bright green smear, and scraps of sunlight stabbing through the trees.

Then I saw a flickering blue light. Just like the one I'd seen from the top of Devil's Thumb. For a second I thought the flicker must mean a migraine was coming on.

"What's wrong?" Cheese asked.

"Can you see that?" I asked.

"See what?"

"The blue light."

"Seriously? Again? Where?"

I turned my head and the sparkling light shifted position, which meant it wasn't in my head but in the real world.

"Right over there," I said, walking toward it.

"You're going the wrong way," said Cheese.

"No I'm not," I called back.

I kept going, pushing my way through the woods. The light was getting brighter. After a few moments, it filled my entire field of vision. My heart beat faster, and I had this weird seasick feeling, like I was sinking down into the earth.

Calm down, I told myself. Count backwards from twenty. *Twenty . . . nineteen . . . eighteen . . . seventeen . . .*

Then I remembered something Mom had told me. "When your head starts spinning," she'd said, "think about your music."

I thought about my favourite song. It's got no bass line to speak of, but OMG it's got horns. It's called "Sir Duke" and it's only 4 minutes long, but it's 4 minutes of hoverboards and high-fives. I played the song all the way through in my mind. And then I heard Cheese say, "Well, thar she blows! Mislaid Lake."

I opened my eyes. The flashing had stopped. A huge stretch of open water lay in front of me.

"This is Mislaid Lake?" I asked.

"That's what the sign says."

Cheese pointed at a tree, where I guess a sign was nailed.

"Good name," I said. "Considering how hard it was to find."

The lake was eerily silent. There weren't any motorboats or pounding boom boxes.

"Can you see the floating island?"

"No," said Cheese. "But I do see a rowboat."

CHAPTER 6

The Department of High-Fives

Seconds until school: 1,796,400
Until Lights Out: 140,702,400

Up until last December, when he pulled me out of Drag River, most kids at my school thought Cheese was a loser.

He got his nickname from saying cheesy things. Like the time he suggested our class write letters to the senior citizens at Linwell Acres. "When they write back, we can turn their letters into a school musical," he said. "Old people have lots of wisdom to share."

#foreheadsmack

Cheese's taste in music was equally weird. He liked to listen to Mozart and Beethoven and stuff. His ring tone was something called "Carnival of the Animals." And he was into Christian metal, which is a whole other level of weird.

Oh, and Cheese was a total spoilsport when it came to following rules. Which could be annoying when you were trying to have fun.

"We can't just *steal* someone's boat," he said. "What if the owner comes along?"

I stepped into the back of the boat. It was full of rainwater.

I found a plastic margarine container and started bailing.

"Nobody's used it for days," I said. "Come on, where's your sense of adventure?"

"Subservient to my sense of honour."

Subservient?

"No way am I getting in that boat," he went on. "Not without a PFD."

"A what?" I said.

"Personal flotation device."

Stupidly, we'd left our life jackets in the canoe. "C'mon," I said. "Help me bail this thing."

He didn't budge. Just stood there on the dock.

"You know I don't swim," he said. "If the boat tips, I'm pooched."

"We won't tip," I said. "There isn't any wind."

The lake was smoother than the screen on my Android. I couldn't see any flashing lights. "Besides," I said, "I've got my Bronze Star, remember? If you fall in, I promise to save you."

Cheese said nothing, but I knew what he was thinking. He was wondering if, in a drowning situation, I'd be able to find him.

I kept bailing. "Do you want to find that island or not?" I asked.

"Of course," he said. "But I also want a rainbow-barfing unicorn to bake me cookies. Doesn't mean it's going to happen."

I sloshed some water at his legs, making him jump.

"Well, I'm going," I said, tossing the bailer into the bottom of the boat. "And I need you to be my eyes. If you don't come, I'll probably get lost."

It was the first time I'd used the blind card with a friend.

I climbed onto the dock and untied the bowline.

Cheese stood there with his hands crossed over his chest.

"Last chance," I said, climbing into the middle seat. "If I get lost out there and die, it's all your fault."

Cheese shook his head and stepped into the stern. "I'm ashamed to belong to a species this simple," he muttered.

I laughed and fitted the oars into the oarlocks. Cheese sat down and fished an egg sandwich out of his knapsack. He ate it while I rowed up the bay. High cliffs rose up on both shores, and I could hear hawks screeching above.

Cheese pulled the binoculars out of his knapsack.

"See anything?" I asked.

"No."

After 10 minutes, we reached the middle of the lake. Four other bays fanned out in different directions. Cheese looked one way, and then the other. Something flashed off to my right.

"What about over there?" I said.

Cheese swung around. "No," he said. "Oh wait, yes."

He was looking up the western bay, perpendicular to the way we'd come. "That is really trippy," he said.

"What?"

"It's our island," he said. "But it's smaller than I thought. It's barely the size of a basketball key."

"Describe it," I said.

"There are two trees at one end. Couple of bushes. And it's definitely moving. Man, that's weird."

I could see the island now, too. Its edges were glimmering, like a ripple of energy was shooting through a glass tube.

"It's surrounded by lily pads," Cheese said. "And the ground looks sketchy, like a soggy pancake."

I rowed the boat closer.

"Think it'll hold my weight?" I asked.

"Doubt it," said Cheese. "Look out, it's coming straight at us."

A gust of wind swept across the lake. The island was 20 metres away, then, suddenly, much less. I stuck out an oar to fend it off. Instantly, the wind died away. The island stalled right there beside the rowboat.

"I want to take some pictures," Cheese said. "Row us around to the other side."

I took us around the island. It was so close I could have reached out and touched it.

"Where's the best place to land?" I asked.

"Don't even — " Cheese said.

"Why not?" I said.

"The ground looks too weak," he said. "You'll fall through for sure."

"I'm a good swimmer," I said.

"Doesn't matter," Cheese said. "There's gotta be a huge knot of roots underneath that island. If you get tangled, you'll drown."

I was going to have to do this quickly — before Cheese bashed my brains out with his boring stick. "Don't worry," I said. "This'll only take a second." I aimed the bow of the boat at the island and pulled.

"Finn, don't."

"Ramming speed!" I cried.

Three strokes later, we slid up against the island. I shipped the oars and climbed up to the bow, then swivelled my legs over the gunwale.

"I wash my hands of this enterprise," Cheese said as I pushed my weight forward and gently set my feet down.

Instantly, I heard a metallic *THWUPP* — as if a metal airlock door had been vacuum-sealed shut behind me. Suddenly my eyeballs screamed with pain. And then I started to fall. Like I was in an elevator that had snapped a cable.

I crouched down and wrapped my arms around my knees. I fell at a zillion kilometres per hour. The blue light flickered on and off, and parts of my body felt like they were vanishing and reappearing.

"Whoooaaa — " I moaned.

Relax, I told myself. *It's just a panic attack. You've had panic attacks before, plenty of times.*

Yeah, but they didn't feel anything like this. This wasn't a panic attack. This was a whole other thing . . . I wasn't just imagining that my body was vanishing and reappearing. My arms and legs were *actually vanishing and reappearing!*

Calm down. Count something.

Right — I was good at counting!

Onebottleofpop . . . twobottlesofpop . . . threebottlesofpop . . . fourbottlesofpop . . .

I looked at my right hand and watched it dissolve. Not just my hand. My whole right arm. I tried to move it, but there was nothing to move. No feeling at all below my shoulder.

Fivebottlesofpop . . . sixbottlesofpop . . . sevenbottlesofpop . . . POP!

A minute later, my hand and arm started to reappear. The falling sensation eased. I smelled wet sand and rotting plants.

I suddenly realized that I was lying face down on the ground. I opened my eyes, raised my head and pushed myself to my knees. Something felt *off*. Like, *really off*.

I felt a twisting in my stomach, like I'd swallowed a thumb-tack. *Stand up, Finn,* I told myself.

But I didn't stand up. Instead, I puked.

"Great," I muttered, wiping my face. I staggered to my feet and took a step forward.

Careful, I thought. *The ground is soft.*

Only — the ground *wasn't* soft. It was as firm as a sidewalk. I'd expected it to be as soggy as a slice of cheese pizza, but no.

I glanced back at Cheese. He was staring at the bottom of the rowboat. Behind him, the lake looked like a wrinkled sheet of tinfoil.

"Hey, Cheese," I said. "Are you seeing this?"

He didn't answer. Didn't even look up. The whole world was yellow-rinsed and silent.

"I'm gonna go and check out those trees," I said.

Still nothing. Not even a smile.

"Be that way," I said, and I walked over to the birch tree. Then I stopped and felt that weird twist in my stomach. Beyond the trees, the island opened up onto a cornfield. Beyond the cornfield, I could see purple hills.

Whoa. Mindfreak. This wasn't possible. Me and Cheese had just rowed *around* the island — hadn't we?

Apparently not. This wasn't an island after all. It was connected to the mainland. How could Cheese and I have possibly missed that? Heck, it *wasn't* possible . . .

I stood there for a moment, staring at the birch tree. Delicate brown veins ran through its oval leaves. The grey-ish sunlight hit each leaf in a slightly different way, creating a kaleidoscope of yellows. I was blown away by how *many* leaves were on the branches. I'd come to think of leaves as one big thing; a giant green *skin* the trees slip into every spring. I'd sort of forgotten that trees actually have *millions* of leaves.

It was weird — like my eyes were dying of thirst and those leaves were a tall, delicious glass of water.

That's when it hit me. I suddenly realized what was different. I felt like I'd drunk five energy drinks.

For the first time in years, I could see *individual* leaves. My vision was back. *I could actually see.*

This isn't real. This can't be happening.

I swung around and looked back at the rowboat. It was 5 metres away, but I could read the letters on its hull. *Lurch,* it was called. I looked at Cheese. He was still staring at the bottom of the boat.

"Hey, Cheese!" I shouted.

He didn't react. He was still ignoring me. *He has an overbite,* I thought. I hadn't noticed that before.

I looked down the narrow bay we'd just paddled. My eyes were drawn to the massive rock walls on both sides. Huge fault lines ran diagonally down the nearest cliff, and stubby cedars grew out of the cracks. Hawks were circling up above. No, wait a second, they *weren't.* Their wings were outstretched as if they were soaring, but they were actually frozen in mid-air.

Head exploding! Head exploding!

I looked back at the lake. The water should've been splashing against the shore. But it wasn't moving at all. The whole scene looked like a sculpture.

I walked back to the rowboat. Cheese was still sitting in the stern.

"Hey," I said.

Still no response.

I looked across the water at the little dock. My heart skipped a beat. Somebody was standing on the shore.

"Whoa, Cheese, check it out!"

I couldn't make out any features, even with my *New! Improved! Vision!* Whoever was there was looking right at us. Weirdly, Cheese kept staring down at his shoes.

"We gotta go, Cheese," I said. "I think we've been busted."

He didn't budge.

"CHEESE!" I shouted.

Still nothing. I knelt down and stared at Cheese's face. That's when I saw the vein in his neck.

He didn't have a pulse. He wasn't ignoring me. He was dead.

CHAPTER 7

The Stroke Victim

Seconds until school: 1,785,600
Until Lights Out: 140,691,600

I jumped back into the boat to grab my phone. I had to call 9-1-1 — fast.

The second I stepped off the island, I heard a metallic *THWUPP*, and my eyesight dropped back down to zero.

For a moment, I felt unsteady. I sat down and grabbed the edge of the bow seat for balance.

"You okay, buddy?" said a voice.

I squinted toward the stern. Everything was bright and blurry. The rowboat drifted away from the island.

"You okay?" the voice said again.

It was Cheese. I shifted to the middle seat.

"You're breathing," I gasped.

"Uh — yeah," he said. "It's . . . um . . . part of my healthy lifestyle. Why?"

I grabbed my knapsack, then let it go. I guess I didn't need to call 9-1-1 after all.

"You didn't have a pulse," I said. "The vein in your neck . . . I saw it . . . You were, well, you looked . . . dead."

"I did?" said Cheese.

I stared at him. "How'd you learn to hold your breath like that?" I asked.

"Like what?" said Cheese.

"Like just now. You held your breath for a minute at least."

"What are you talking about?" Cheese said. "You only rammed the island, like, ten seconds ago."

I didn't know what to say to that. Cheese didn't sound like he was joking.

"Good call not to go ashore," he said. "The island wouldn't hold your weight. I doubt it'd even support me."

I looked back at the island. The wind was blowing it sideways.

What just happened? Did I lose consciousness or something? Was I having some sort of hallucination?

"What's happened to your shirt?" Cheese asked.

I looked down. "Where?"

"Under your chin. That yellow stain."

I felt my shirt. It was wet from when I'd puked. I pulled it up to my nose. Yep, smelled like puke.

"You okay?" said Cheese. "You look pale."

I stared at the island. It was still glowing around the edges.

"Cheese, I need to ask you something," I said.

"Shoot."

How could I say it without sounding crazy? *Had* I really climbed out of the boat? Seen a cornfield?

"Look at the island and tell me. It's an island, right? Like, it's not connected to the mainland?"

Cheese didn't bother looking at the island. "You do remember that we paddled *around* it, right?"

"Yeah," I said. "But that doesn't mean . . . "

Cheese looked right at me. "It doesn't mean what?"

Maybe I hit my head, I thought. *Maybe I even had a concussion.*

"Are you sure you're okay?" Cheese asked. "You seem like you're having a stroke."

"I'm not having a stroke," I said.

"How do you know? I bet you don't even know the symptoms."

"What are they?"

"Tingling in your arms or legs, difficulty speaking, sometimes one side of your face droops."

"I'm not feeling any of that," I said.

"Do you feel dizzy? Confused? Having any trouble with your vision?"

"That pretty much sums up my whole life," I said.

"Are you having *more* trouble than usual, I mean?" Cheese asked.

I shrugged.

Cheese leaned forward and checked my pupils. Then he sat back again. "We better go back," he said. We switched seats and he set the oars in the oarlocks. "If your symptoms persist . . . well, let's just hope they don't."

I watched Cheese row. He turned the boat around and started pulling for the dock.

I twisted around and looked one last time at the island. It was mostly a blur, but I could still see the pulsing light. Little waves slapped against the side of the boat. A hundred thoughts filled my head.

Reasons I Must've Made It Up:
-I've lost half my vision
-Eyes don't just heal themselves
-I have a history of panic attacks
-I haven't had much sleep

I decided I must've hit my head somehow. But that didn't explain the puke stain on my shirt . . .

Suddenly I remembered something else. "Hey, Cheese," I said. "Is anyone standing by the dock? I thought I saw someone standing over there."

"Seriously?" said Cheese. He turned around. Then he said, "Holy cow." He let go of the oars.

"What?" I said.

"Hang on." He reached for the binoculars. The oar blades floated in the water. The boat drifted sideways.

"You greasebag," Cheese said. He dropped the binoculars into his lap. "You've been lying about your eyes," he said.

I made a little O shape with my mouth. "There's actually someone there?" I said.

"Don't play me," he said. "You know there is. You're the one with X-ray vision."

"I don't have X-ray vision," I said. "Things just got really clear when I was on the island."

"Yeah, that makes a *lot* of sense," said Cheese. "Considering you never got out of the boat."

What was that supposed to mean? Of course I got out of the boat.

Cheese grabbed the oars again and started pulling. He didn't speak again until we reached the dock.

CHAPTER
8

Tab

Seconds until school: 1,784,700
Until Lights Out: 140,690,700

The good news is, I wasn't having a stroke. I really had seen someone standing by the dock. She was still there when we landed and tied up. She stepped into the sunshine and I saw the blaze of her face.

"You're the girl from last night," Cheese said.

"Sorry?" she said.

"You paddled past our dock."

I finished tying the stern line and stood up.

"Where was that?" the girl said.

"In Pancake Bay," said Cheese. "I spoke to you in French."

"Oh right," she said. "You called me *madame*."

I couldn't see it, but I could *hear* Cheese blushing. The girl turned to me. "About that staring problem you've got."

Crap. I thought I'd been looking at the ground. I looked away. It felt like she'd punched me in the throat.

"FYI," she said, "you shouldn't steal people's boats. The owner would go ballistic if he found out."

Her voice was raspy; pebbles rubbed together.

"We didn't steal anything," said Cheese. "We just borrowed it for a few minutes."

The girl put something on her head. It looked like a bike helmet. "If that makes it okay in your books, then whatever," she said.

I realized I hadn't said a single word. Had she been following us? Why else would she be here?

Cheese sighed. "Look, this is silly," he said. "We messed up. We get it. We don't want to be enemies. Peace?"

The wind blew through the trees. The girl kicked something near the ground. It made a whirring noise. I turned my head sideways to get a better view.

"Sure," she said. "Whatever you say."

She was leaning against a bike. She made that whirring noise again. It was a bike pedal she was kicking.

"How'd you get that bike out here?" I asked.

Yay — I'd said something! Only seven syllables, but still.

"Uh, I rode on the Organ Donor," she said. "Duh."

"The what?" said Cheese.

"Seriously?" she said. "You guys don't know about the Organ Donor?"

Cheese and I looked at each other.

"It's a trail," she said. She spun her pedal again. Then she added, "Nice shirt, by the way."

She was talking to Cheese.

"Thanks," he said.

"I have all eight seasons on DVD," she said.

"Seriously?" said Cheese.

"Yeah. Remember the episode when they cut off Uncle Jesse's mullet?"

"Best TV mullet ever," said Cheese.

Mullets? On My Little Pony?

"Did you see the episode where Joey's old girlfriend calls him up and wants to get back together?"

"Classic," said Cheese. "What about the one where D.J. and Stephanie get handcuffed together?"

"YES!" said the girl. "Season two, episode nineteen."

"Are you guys serious?" I said. "Isn't *My Little Pony* for kids?"

Neither of them said anything right away.

"We're not talking about *My Little Pony,*" the girl said.

"You're not?" I said.

"We're talking about *Full House,*" Cheese said.

"It's on his shirt, see?" said the girl. "*Full House.*"

Great, I thought. *She thinks I'm an idiot.*

Cheese slapped a mosquito and didn't say anything.

"So," the girl went on. "You guys are staying on Pancake Bay?"

"Yeah," said Cheese. "Finn's parents have a place."

"Who's Finn?"

"Me."

"Oh. Hi."

"Hi," I said.

My eyelid was twitching. Rapid bursts of three or four.

"I'm Tab," she said.

"I'm Cheese."

"Seriously? Cheese?"

"Yeah. It's a nickname. My real name's Jeevan."

"Cool," she said. "Hey, these bugs are brutal here. You guys want to walk? You're heading home anyway, right?"

Cheese nodded, so Tab hoisted her bike over her shoulder. Then she started hiking up the hill.

"But we came from that direction," said Cheese, pointing into the forest.

"Trust me," said Tab. "This way's faster."

Cheese followed her up the hill, and I followed Cheese. *He must have two shirts the same colour,* I thought. *I could've sworn it was his* My Little Pony *shirt.*

I was starting to get sweaty, and I could hear Cheese panting when Tab stopped walking and set her bike down on the ground. *Wow,* I thought, *she carried that bike all this time. She's either really strong, or the bike has an ultralight frame. Maybe both.*

"Here we go," she said. "The Organ Donor."

At one time it must've been a logging road, since there were two deep ruts along the outer edges. Since then, lots of people must have been through on bikes and carved a single-track trail into the centre.

I thought Tab might hop on her bike and ride away, but she didn't. The trail wasn't wide enough for all three of us, so Cheese walked beside her and I trailed behind. It really sucks to be the loser who has to walk behind, but after the past five months at school, I was getting used to it.

We turned left. There were sharp spikes in the trail, and some hairpin turns. A few places where I'd have liked to build ramps.

"That's a nice bike," I said once, trying to join in.

"Thanks," said Tab.

"What is it, a Haro?"

"No," she said. "It's a Trek. See there? *Trek.*"

She pointed at the logo on the frame.

"Right," I said.

I didn't say anything for a while after that. I'd made a fool of myself twice, and I didn't want to do it again. The trail swerved back and forth, and I counted my steps. Mom says I count because I'm OCD, but lately I've been doing it for other reasons. Like, I've started counting telephone poles and driveways and newspaper boxes. Things that help me find my way around.

There are big holes in my vision now. Like, the houses on Cheese's street look mostly the same, and there's no way I can see the numbers from the sidewalk. But if I keep track of the number of driveways I walk past, then I can usually find my way.

Anyway, I was counting my steps, and when I got to 2,350, the trail crossed a little meadow, and we were blasted with sunlight. I put on my sunglasses and saw something off to the left, above the treeline. I figured it was the cellphone tower we'd passed earlier in the day.

A couple of minutes later, the trail went down a hill and spat us out on a grassy lawn.

"That's my place, over there," said Tab, pointing. A flash of blue lake glinted between the trees.

The journey out to Mislaid Lake had taken close to 2 hours. The return trip to Tab's only took us 30 minutes.

We walked across the lawn and stood in the shade of some trees. A big animal came bounding up the lawn.

"Watch out," said Tab. "He's epically farty. His bowels are vast caverns of flesh-melting stink."

It was a big yellow dog. It ran a wide circle around us and

then plowed straight into Tab's stomach. "Oof!" she cried. "Skyforce, heel!"

The dog's named Skyforce? Who names their dog Skyforce?

"Hey, Skyforce!" I said.

The dog turned suddenly and leapt up on me, tail wagging.

"Skyforce, DOWN!" Tab shouted.

The dog's front paws were on my shoulders. The two of us were doing this weird human-doggy dance.

"I said DOWN!"

Skyforce licked my chin and jumped down. He kept running around us. He was a blur of yellow-gold.

"So," said Tab. "You guys like swimming?"

Cheese didn't answer. "Sure," I said.

"What about heights? You okay with heights?"

"He is," said Cheese. "How come?"

"There are some epic jumping rocks not far from here. If you come back tomorrow we could ride up there and check them out."

Cheese glanced at me for a moment, and then back at Tab. "What do you mean, *ride*?" he asked.

"On bikes," said Tab. "What did you think I meant?"

Cheese glanced at me again. "We don't have bikes up here," he said.

"No problem," said Tab. "We have extras in the shed. We'd have to lower the seats to fit you guys, but that's easy."

"Er . . . we may have plans tomorrow," Cheese said. "Right, Finn?" He poked me in the ribs.

"Uh, right," I said. *We have plans? What plans?*

"But you never know," Cheese said. "Maybe we can wiggle

out of them. Give me your coordinates and I can let you know in the morning."

Tab nodded and the two of them traded phones and spent a few seconds adding each other to their contacts.

"Viveganthanan?" Tab said. "What is it, Sri Lankan?" Cheese nodded. "That's what I thought. I like the way it sounds."

He grinned so massively even I could see it.

Tab didn't ask for my phone.

* * *

A few minutes later we were paddling back home across the lake.

"Do you think Tab is short for something?" I asked. "Like Tabitha?"

Cheese shrugged.

"Or maybe it stands for something," I said. "Like, Toronto Association for the Blind. Or Toledo Area Bicyclists."

Cheese laughed. "Somehow I don't think so," he said.

"Turtle Aquatic Box," I said. "Tuck Aero-Bars."

"What are Tuck Aero-Bars?" Cheese asked.

"Handlebar extensions," I said. "The best in the world. They let you lean forward, like an Olympic cyclist."

Cheese picked something, a spider maybe, out of the canoe, and flicked it into the lake. "Nobody names their kids after bike gear," he said.

The afternoon sun sparkled on the water and stung my eyes. *T-A-B*, I thought. *Thanks A Bunch*.

"So, I have a question," said Cheese, turning around.

"Hit me," I said.

He rested his paddle across the gunwales. "That thing that happened back on Mislaid Lake. When you somehow saw Tab. Which, as we know, is impossible."

"It's not impossible," I said. "There's something truly weird about that island."

Cheese turned his head and looked at the south shore. "How would you know? I mean, you never even got out of the boat."

It was my turn to take a break from paddling.

"Yes I did," I said. "You just didn't notice because you were playing dead."

Cheese scratched his arm. "I didn't play dead," he said.

"You did, too," I said.

The canoe pivoted sideways in the breeze.

"You have to believe me," I said.

"I'm trying," Cheese said.

It didn't sound like he was trying very hard.

"You were hunched over," I said. "You were staring at your flip-flops. You stayed like that, frozen, for a minute at least."

Cheese shook the drops of water off his paddle. "Sooo, if you had perfect vision back there," he said, "why did you think I was wearing a *My Little Pony* T-shirt?"

Seriously? I have to answer this question? Both shirts are the same colour, and I just assumed . . .

I dipped my fingers into the lake and traced a figure eight on the thwart. It glistened and then faded in the sunshine. "You have to believe me," I said again.

Cheese tapped his paddle against the gunwale. "I guess I believe that you believe," he said.

He looked at me for a couple of seconds — at least, I *think* he was looking at me. Finally he turned around and started paddling again. I put my paddle in the water, too.

"So, what about tomorrow?" he asked.

"Simple," I said. "We accompany Tab to the jumping rocks."

"Right," said Cheese. "But what about the bikes?"

"She said she had extras in her shed."

Cheese turned around. "You're *not* serious," he said.

"Sure I am. Why?"

"You can't *see*."

"I know," I said. "But I'll figure something out. She's the only girl for five hundred kilometres. We can't waste this opportunity."

T-A-B, I thought, *Totally Amazing Biker.*

"But what if you crash into a tree?" Cheese asked.

"Relax," I said. "Trees are green and grey. The trail is brown. I'll stick to the brown."

"But what about the roots and rocks? What about, you know, *cliffs*?"

"Just wear that neon yellow T-shirt you've got. I can see that. I'll ride right behind you."

"I can't wear that shirt in front of Tab," said Cheese.

"Why not?" I said.

"It's a hand-me-down from my sister. It's a girl's shirt. Can't we just tell Tab about your eyes?"

"No way," I said. "That'd just be a turnoff. Besides, she'd never let me ride one of their bikes if she knew I might crash it."

Cheese tapped the side of the canoe with his paddle.

"Wear the ugly yellow shirt," I said. "Just turn it inside out so Tab won't see the design. I'll stay right behind you. What's the worst that could happen?"

CHAPTER
9

Splitsville

Seconds until school: 1,778,400
Until Lights Out: 140,684,400

You know how when you exercise really hard, and your clothes get all gross and sweaty, and you try to take them off, but you're so tired you only get halfway done, and then you lie down on the floor, all tangled up in your dumb clothes, and you just hang out down there on the floor for a while?

Me and Cheese had hammered it coming home. Dropped a total pain bomb on ourselves. But after we tied up the canoe and climbed the steps to Splitsville, I heard Dad laughing with his friends, and then I suddenly got real tired.

I snuck through the back door and went into my bedroom and that's when I wound up lying on the floor. I could hear Dad and his buddies telling fishing stories outside. I stared up at the collection of sticky notes on my wall.

Things That I Will Never Get to Do:
–drive a car
–visit Brazil
–do a Superman no-hander on my bike

–get a girlfriend
–be normal

I sighed and checked my phone for the time. It was just after 6 p.m. I did a quick calculation: 20 days and 14 hours left until school.

So . . . 20 days x 24 hours x 60 minutes x 60 seconds = 1,728,000

Plus 14 hours x 60 minutes x 60 seconds = 50,400

Add them together: 1,778,400 seconds

Now 1,778,399.

Now 1,778,398.

My stomach did a somersault. Time was running out — fast.

More laughter from outside. Smoke drifted through the window. Dad was grilling fish on the barbecue.

I thought about the trail Tab had shown us. The Organ Donor. Cheese was right — it had a lot of rocks and roots. I'd played it cool in front of Cheese, but I was actually pretty scared. It had been eight months since I'd done my Evel Knievel act at Drag River. I could still feel the shock of unexpectedly sailing off the cliff . . .

Welcome aboard FinnAir, flight 001, bound for the bottom of the Drag River watershed. Estimated flying time: 2.5 seconds. Please stow all carry-on items under your seat, or in one of the overhead bins. In the extremely likely event of an emergency over water, your seat cushion may be used as a flotation device. Just slip your arms through the straps, hugging the cushion to your chest as shown on the safety information card . . .

My own fault. I'd had plenty of clues. All those spills I'd

taken over the last two years. All the boulders that appeared in my path out of nowhere. Breaking my collarbone when I went to CrankWorx with the Skid Marks.

Looking back, it's so obvious about my eyes. Why hadn't I noticed? Why hadn't my parents noticed?

Cut yourself a break, Finn. Not even the cops noticed.

True story. One day I was cruising down Martindale Road and a cop turned on his *FWOOP-FWOOP* lights behind me.

I stopped my bike. Cop got out of his car. "What's the big idea?" he growled.

Turned out I'd blown straight through a stop sign. Of course, the cop had been sitting right there.

I hadn't seen him *or* the stop sign.

"You're a vehicle, just like a car," said the cop.

He stared at me with his angry cop stare. The lights on the police car were flashing and everything.

"That's a seventy-five dollar ticket," he said. "Have you got an extra seventy-five dollars lying around?"

"No," I said truthfully. "I just — I didn't see the sign."

"It's new," said the policeman. "Just went up a week ago. But that's no excuse not to stop. It's a dangerous intersection."

The cop stared at me, hoping I'd say something.

"You're lucky a car didn't hit you," he went on. "And I'm glad to see you're wearing a helmet. You've got some sense, at least."

A group of kids appeared on their bikes. They slowed down, stopped at the intersection and then rode past. I think I might have been crying a little. I could hear one of the boys snickering.

"Okay," the cop said. "I won't give you a ticket this time.

Just be more careful, okay? We don't want you to get killed."

I nodded. The cop got into his car and drove away. I walked my bike the rest of the way to school.

"You are the luckiest dude ever," Spencer said when I told him.

"Your dad would've killed you if he found out," said Minnow.

No, he would've done something worse. I know this because, later on, he actually did it.

I hitched my legs up on my bed and noticed a column of sticky notes beside my dresser. It was a list of names I'd started the night before. I reached back and peeled them off and held them up to my face.

Storm Vitreous

Rod Macula

Jettison Black

I'd been thinking about changing my name. Those were my three leading candidates. Vitreous, Rod and Macula are all parts of the eye. Jettison Black (Jett for short) is just a cool-sounding name.

I hadn't told my parents about the name change yet. They'd just get all freaked out about it. Dad especially. He'd be all, *Where's your family pride?*

Don't have any, I'd tell him. *You bashed it out of me.*

I stuck the notes back on the wall and thought about growing my hair long. Or shaving it off altogether. It didn't matter. Anything to become someone new.

A breeze blew through the open window. Dad laughed again and I heard him crack a handful of walnuts.

I remembered the first time I heard him cracking those

walnuts. It was the night I got home from the hospital. I went to the garage and found my dirt jumper missing. At first I thought someone had broken in and stolen it. Then I realized. It was Dad.

"Time to find a new hobby," he said, after I'd tracked him down in front of the TV. "That thing nearly killed you."

I yelled at him then. Really yelled. "I bought that bike *with my own money*! I put those new shocks on *by hand*!"

Dad didn't answer. Didn't even bother to fight back. Arguing with him was like throwing snowballs at a snowdrift.

"How would you like it if I gave away your *car*?" I shouted.

"Ha," said Dad. "You'd be doing me a favour. Bank owns it anyway. Go right ahead."

With that, he cracked a handful of walnuts and turned the hockey game up.

"The Skid Marks need me," I yelled. "They can't win at CrankWorx without me!"

"You are *not* going to CrankWorx," my father said.

End of discussion.

And then, after what Dr. Zhang told us, it got even worse.

"We'll get you a tandem bike," said Dad.

Ugh. A bicycle built for two? No way! I liked riding solo. I wasn't a passenger.

"Acceptance isn't an easy thing," said Dad. "It's a gnarly trail, full of roots and rocks. But you'll have to face it eventually, Finn. You can't keep doing all the things you used to do. It's just not safe."

Blah, blah, blah. I covered my ears and stormed away. Then I went into the kitchen and appealed to my mom.

I found her drinking coffee outside on the back porch. She

looked like an antique vase, covered in cracks. "You and Dad don't trust me," I said.

"Not true," she said. "It's your *eyes* we don't trust."

Still, she and Dad must've felt a bit guilty, since they bought me a stationary bike.

What a laugh. A bike that didn't move. Total waste of heartbeats.

Didn't they know? I biked for the danger. For the joy of catching air. For that moment when you almost lose control, then pedal like crazy and pull yourself out of the hole.

I never even took the thing out of the box. And I never saw my dirt jumper again.

There was another burst of laughter on the deck outside, so I stood up and finished getting changed. Then I went outside. Cheese was reading a book in the hammock. My dad turned around.

"Finn!" he cried. "Where ya been, buddy?"

"Around."

He was standing with two guys. They both had red faces. They were wearing baggy dad-shorts and holding brown bottles.

"Morty, Bill, this is my son, Finn."

Deer: them. Headlights: me.

I could tell that Dad had told them the story. They knew about my eyes and had no idea what to say.

"Hey," said one.

"Yo," said the other.

I couldn't blame them. I wouldn't know what to say either. *Hey kid, total downer about going blind . . .*

Dad clacked his tongs together and took a sip of his drink. I headed inside but he stopped me first.

"You wanted to know about tussocks," he said.

"I did?" I said.

"That's what your mother said."

Oh, right! Tussocks = floating islands.

"You didn't find one, did you?" said Dad.

"No," I said, glancing at Cheese. "It's just . . . We saw the word in a book. We got confused."

Dad used the tongs to flip something on the grill. "They're great habitat for fish," he said. "Minnows spawn in the root system, which attracts larger fish. There's a rumour going around that there's a tussock somewhere in these lakes. If you boys come across it — "

"Sure," I said. "We'll let you know."

The bald guy in a green shirt asked where the little boy's room was. "Inside to the left," said Dad. "And grab me another ginger ale while you're at it."

He went inside and a moment later we heard a flush, and the whole cabin shook from the vibration of the pipes.

"Hey," Dad said, "what do you say to some pickerel? Fresh off the boat. You boys interested?"

"Not really," I said. "I'm vegetarian, remember?"

"I know, but I thought I could tempt you this one time. You must be sick of quinoa salad."

"Not really," I said.

"I'm in!" Cheese called out from the hammock.

"Attaboy," Dad said.

* * *

Late that night, a big storm moved in. A storm so huge it lasted two days. Thirteen centimetres of rain fell over forty-eight hours. It was a new record, the radio said.

Since there wasn't any Wi-Fi, and we didn't have an Xbox, Cheese and I spent all our time playing card games and Yahtzee.

In lockdown, Cheese texted Tab.

Me, too, she texted back. *Tomorrow?*

When we got sick of playing games, Cheese would pick up a book and I'd go into my room to work on my lists. I wrote down everything I knew about the floating island.

It has two trees.

It glows.

It's not really an island at all.

I sighed and crumpled up the list. Nothing about it made any sense. What had happened to my eyes? Why had they worked there, but not here?

It wasn't a dream, I thought. I'd seen Tab at the dock, half a kilometre away. That wasn't a lucky guess. Even Cheese admitted that.

Not a stroke, not a hallucination. Something weird was happening on that island. But what?

I needed to go back and find out — soon.

CHAPTER
10

The Organ Donor

Seconds until school: 1,555,200
Until Lights Out: 140,461,200

It was still drizzling when we got up the next morning. I shuffled into the living room and glared out the window: 18 days left. I did the calculations . . . *1,555,200 seconds left.*

The forest looked as grey as smoke. Like someone had taken a straw and sucked all the colour out of the world.

Cheese came out of his bedroom and flopped onto the beanbag chair.

A shred of colour drifted past the window. For a moment I saw cedars, green and shaggy with rain. Then the fog closed in again.

"If I play any more Yahtzee," I said, "I will probably have to eat poison."

We'd actually run out of Yahtzee scorecards and started drawing our own. That's how bad things had got.

Cheese's phone vibrated. He tapped it to life.

"Tab?" I asked.

"Yeah," he said.

He sat forward and read the text.

"She's texting you a lot," I said. *Don't sound jealous. Don't sound jealous.*

"She wants to know if we're coming over."

"In this weather?" I said.

Cheese typed a message back. A minute later his phone vibrated again.

"Hmmm," he said.

"What?" I asked.

He handed me the phone. "Nice picture, eh?"

"What's with the glam clothes?" I asked.

"She was in a fashion show," said Cheese.

"Seriously?" I asked.

"She's pretty, hey? Pretty as a song."

Right there. That's a classic Cheese statement. *Pretty as a song.* That's how he got his nickname.

I gave him back his phone and we went and had breakfast. By the time we were finished, the drizzling had stopped and the fog was lifting. Cheese went outside and looked down at the lake. "Motorboat's gone," he said.

I wrote a note for my mom, who still wasn't awake, while Cheese changed. When he came back out, he was wearing the ugly yellow T-shirt.

* * *

It took longer to cross the lake this time, since Cheese spent the whole trip texting instead of paddling.

Almst thr, he wrote.

I C U, Tab texted back.

He texted: *Prple boathouse?*

She replied: *Grn bkini!*

That got his attention. Instantly, Cheese gave me a new

heading. We paddled for 10 minutes and then I heard Tab's voice bouncing across the water.

"Bom dia!" she shouted.

"Bonjour, mademoiselle!"

"Vem aqui! Vem aqui!"

The green bikini thing turned out to be a joke. She was wearing cut-off jean shorts and an aggressively ugly Homer Simpson T-shirt. Cheese, of course, was all over that. He knows every single line that Homer ever uttered.

"Donuts . . . " he said, in his best Homer drawl. "Is there anything they can't do?"

"Shut up, brain," said Tab, "or I'll stab you with a Q-Tip!"

The two of them exploded into laughter. *Great,* I thought. *That's how the day is going to go.*

Just then Skyforce came bounding down the lawn. I rolled around with him on the grass until Tab suddenly grabbed my hand and pulled me up.

"Come on," she said, "you need to meet the parentals. Play nice, okay? Or else they won't let me go."

The three of us ran up to the cottage. Skyforce trailed behind.

Tab's parents were nice, but her dad was intense. He wanted to know what music I was into. He name-dropped a bunch of feeble bands, like K-Rino and Sage Francis, which made me want to laugh, but I didn't. I asked him if he'd heard of MPSQ. He said no. After that the conversation sort of stalled.

Tab's mom was cooler. She'd been picking blueberries all morning. She'd blended up a smoothie that was, to quote Cheese, "a beacon of deliciousness."

Tab's dad laughed and said, "Easy, don't lay it on too thick."

Then he put his hands on his hips and told Tab she was free to go.

Tab led us to the tool shed, where the bikes were stored. "These extras belong to my brothers," she said, yanking open the metal door. "But they're away on exchange, so they'll never know."

A badminton net was tangled in the spokes, but Tab separated it all and dragged the bikes into the sunshine.

"There's a purple one and a red one," she said. "Who wants which?"

"Purple!" said Cheese.

"Here you go."

"Yes!" said Cheese.

Great, I thought, *what am I getting stuck with?*

"The red one's not much to look at," said Tab. "My brother got the frame second-hand, and put the gears and brakes and stuff on by himself."

I lifted the frame to check the weight. It was heavier than my old Ironhorse, that's for sure. I spun the wheel. "Tires need inflating," I said. "But other than that, it looks serviceable."

I knelt down and ran my hand along the carbon lay-up. It was a Snakebite Vengeance, a hardtail, nothing special. Spencer had a Snakebite, too, but his was the Venom, which was a couple of models better. It had full suspension on both wheels, and, best of all, a dropper post.

"How's that working for you?" Tab asked.

"Working fine," I said, standing up and throwing my leg over the top tube. I rested on the saddle and checked out the hardware. It had eleven speeds, and a mid-level shifter and brakes.

"It's really just a beater," Tab explained. "He keeps his real ride back at home. It's worth a couple thousand dollars, easy."

Cheese crouched down and started pumping up his tires.

"Wait here," said Tab. "I'll grab the Allen key for the seats." She ran back to the house while Cheese kept pumping. I leaned forward on the bars, rocking the bike back and forth. I could practically hear the hum of the thick tread tires on the dirt. I pictured myself spinning the crank.

"You're really sure you want to do this?" Cheese asked, looking up.

I nodded, even though my stomach was in knots. I knew my head could be knocked off at any time once we started down that trail.

"Stay *right* behind me," Cheese warned.

"I will," I said. "Don't stop unless it gets gnarly."

"Like if we come to a neck-breaking cliff?" said Cheese.

"Yeah." I smiled. "I've had enough hospital visits for one year."

Cheese finished inflating his tires and moved over to start on mine. I climbed down off the bike as Tab reappeared. She used the Allen key to lower both of our seats. I finished pumping up my rear tire while Cheese used a bungee cord to strap his life jacket to his rear rack.

"Why are you bringing that?" Tab asked.

"In case we come across any more rowboats."

Finally we were all set to go. We clipped on our helmets. "Ready to donate some organs?" Tab cried.

"*Must* you use that phrase?" said Cheese.

Tab hooted. "Don't worry. It's not as bad as it sounds."

I cranked the grip of my handlebar as if it was a motocross throttle. "*Braap braap!*" I shouted. "Let's get this show on the road!"

Tab throttled up, too. *"Braap braap braaaaaaaap!"*

She blasted across the lawn and disappeared into a hole in the forest. We followed her into the hole and the trail curved left. I leaned the bike left and felt it roll comfortably beneath me.

Up ahead, I heard Cheese's wheels slishing through greasy mud. Then I was in the grease, too, and my back wheel was slipping sideways. Cheese moved onto the grassy ridge between the two wheel ruts. That was better — more traction there.

OMG. This is crazy. What am I doing?

Cheese sped up.

OUCH! Pothole!

Keep your butt in the air, I reminded myself. *And keep the shoulders loose. Lean the bike into the curves.*

We hammered up a hill. I stood up in the pedals and ground it out. Cheese was setting an easy pace, which was about the only thing that kept me from wiping out.

Then suddenly the trail nosed downhill. Cheese's yellow shirt vanished into a sea of yellow wildflowers. The edges of my vision went blurry. The bike machine-gunned down the washboardy hill.

My brain was screaming: *What the heck are you doing? This is the stupidest thing you've ever done, Finn! You could die out here. Die.*

Suddenly, I slid to a stop.

"Braap! Braap!" Cheese hooted.

"Braap! Braap-ap-ap-ap-ap-ap-ap!" Tab cried.

Their voices faded away into the forest.

What the heck was I doing? I'd seen Cheese's shirt for 30 seconds, and then I'd lost it.

I took a few deep breaths. I waited for another minute.

Cheese didn't reappear. He probably hadn't even noticed that I'd stopped.

Come on Finn, I thought. *Don't be such a wuss. You can do this. You're the champion Skid Mark.*

Correction: You *were* the champion Skid Mark. *Were.*

I climbed back onto the bike and slowly started pedalling. A neon yellow stripe blocked the path.

"There you are."

It was Cheese. He'd turned around and come looking for me after all. "You okay?" he asked.

"Yeah," I said, coming to a stop.

"Was I going too fast?" Cheese asked.

"Maybe a bit," I said.

"No problem. I'll slow down. I'm your wingman, so just let me know what you need."

He turned his bike around and we started riding again. His neon shirt was right in front of me.

"Keep right!" Cheese shouted. "There's a downhill here. Bridge at the bottom."

"Cool," I lied, hoping I could keep the bike upright. Cheese stopped pedalling and went into a coast.

For a few moments the trail was as smooth as a sidewalk. The air roared past my ears as we picked up speed. The bike sizzled beneath me. I hit the wooden bridge with a soft *thlump*. The tires hummed on the smooth surface for a moment, and then I was back on crunchy trail.

We charged up another hill. I dropped down a few gears and curled my fingers around the spongy grips. My quads were nearly bursting out of my skin. Ever seen broken springs popping out of a mattress? That was me.

Huff-puff. Huff-puff. When did I get so out of shape?

At the top of the hill, Cheese skidded to a stop. Tab was waiting for us, too, and I pulled in beside her.

"You guys okay?" she asked.

Cheese nodded and sucked in air.

"How's my pace?" she asked.

"Perfect," he gasped.

The sky was clogged with clouds. They were as dark as squished plums.

"The weather can't make up its mind," I said.

Cheese looked up at the sky. "Ladies and gentlemen, we have a storm cell," he said.

A light breeze washed over our faces.

"It's tracking east," said Tab. "It won't hit us."

"Did you hear about that guy who went jogging," Cheese said, "and got hit by lightning *twice*?"

"Over in Grouse Gulch," I said. "Just a few klicks from here."

"He just kept on running, even after he'd been hit," said Cheese. "He ran all the way home."

"If the bone ain't showing," Tab said, "keep on going."

"But the dude got hit *twice*," said Cheese. "What are the odds of that? A million to one? Maybe a billion to one?"

The sun vanished behind the clouds and then came back out again. There was a far-off rumble of thunder. That reminded me of what Cheese had said about tussocks, and how a thunderstorm usually tore them to pieces. I had to get back to the floating island fast — to see if my vision really worked there.

"Hey," said Cheese. "Check this out."

Tab turned around. "Hello, beautiful," she said.

They were looking at something on the tree. I walked over and stood beside them.

"It's a moth," said Cheese, for my benefit.

"Well, *obviously*," Tab said.

I leaned in for a look. It was bigger than my hand. It had yellow-pink wings, with a peacock eye in the centre of each one.

"If this one's a male, it won't even live for a week," said Tab.

"Seriously?" I said.

She nodded. "It has to find itself a mate and fertilize the eggs in four days or so."

"Good thing I'm not a moth," said Cheese. "I've been alive for thirteen years and I haven't even got a girlfriend."

Tab laughed at that. So did I. The moth slowly opened and closed its wings.

"They're nocturnal," Tab went on, "but they can't see well enough in the dark to find a mate. That's why they fly in crazy zigzag patterns. They fly in one direction, take a sniff, then fly in another direction, take another sniff. Eventually the male will find the female."

No way. I'd always thought moths flew like that because they were stupid. They got around with just their sense of smell?

The moth opened its wings and suddenly launched into the air. It spiralled up and up, in a wonky yellow-pink vortex.

"Let's get going," I said. "We don't have all day. *Braap! Braap!*"

We clipped on our helmets and climbed back on the bikes. Tab took off first, then Cheese, then me. The trail twisted and turned. I was getting used to it now.

"Bump!" Cheese yelled back.

I slowed down, and then *FRAAAAAA!* I was pogo-ing over tree roots. If I'd seen that coming, I would've bunny-hopped it, easy.

Groin, meet pain. Pain, meet groin.

"Going down!" Cheese shouted from somewhere up ahead. Great. Now I was riding completely blind.

And yet the bike felt like a part of my body. I'd missed that, and I felt so happy and so alive. I stamped my feet onto the flats and held on. I was at race pace now, and accelerating fast.

Then suddenly Cheese's shirt was dead ahead. I'd been pedalling hard to catch him and now he was right there.

"Hey, buddy!" I said, drawing even and still going hard.

"What are you *doing*?" he shouted as I passed.

I couldn't slow down. "HOOOO-WEEEE!" I cried.

I sent him a lighthouse beam of joy. And then I dug into the pedals and shot farther ahead.

"Hey!" Cheese yelled. "Take it easy!"

He was behind me now, but I didn't care. Flecks of mud spattered my legs and back. The vibrations of the handlebars sent shock waves up my arms. I was going a million kilometres an hour. The air whistled past my ears.

"Look out!" Cheese shouted.

Look out for what? Then I saw it — at the last possible moment. A mud puddle the size of Quebec.

I skidded sideways, sending up a curtain of brown water. My tires sank into the ooze. I pedalled hard, though, and made it through.

I coasted halfway up the other side of the hill. I could hear Cheese somewhere close behind me.

"BAM!" I shouted, spinning the bike around. "That was INCREDIBLE! Did you see that? Man!"

"Oh, noooo," Tab groaned.

She was standing off to the side. She must've seen the puddle in time and gone around.

I took a few deep breaths. I could hear Cheese wading through the water.

"That you, Cheese?" I called down.

"Yeah," he muttered.

He sounded teed off.

"Did I get you?" I said.

Tab snickered. "What are you, *blind*? You totally cut him off. That's why he fell."

Cheese said nothing. He dragged his bike up the hill. Even I could see he was coated in mud.

"Want a towel?" Tab asked.

"No thanks," said Cheese. He peeled off his shirt and wrung it out.

Somehow I'd stayed totally dry. I clicked my brake levers open and shut: *clickety-click*.

"I'm sorry," I said. "I was just trying to catch up, and then I couldn't stop."

"Shut up," said Cheese. "Just . . . don't say anything."

Thunder rattled far away. Cheese scraped gobs of mud off his legs. Then he put his shirt back on. It wasn't yellow anymore. More like dirt brown.

"I'm sorry," I tried again. "But look on the bright side. You didn't like that shirt anyway."

Cheese scooped a handful of mud out of his derailleur. Then he pushed his bike past me. "I'm not communicating with you right now," he said. "Just leave me alone for a few minutes, okay?"

I felt like I'd been stung by a wasp. I hadn't meant to cut him off. It was just an accident.

Cheese and Tab walked side by side, pushing their bikes up the hill. I followed a dozen metres behind.

"Do I look like a tough guy with all this mud?" Cheese asked.

"You look like a manly beast," said Tab.

"Really?" said Cheese.

"Not at all," said Tab. "You look like a shipwreck survivor."

"But a manly one, right?"

"Totally manly."

The two of them laughed and I felt my mind begin to spin. *She likes him better,* I thought. *And no wonder. I am a total bonehead.*

"Want to hear my winning idea?" Cheese said.

"Sure," said Tab.

"You know how pizzas are round or square?" he said. "I want to open a restaurant where the pizzas are *triangular.*"

"Brilliant," said Tab. "Have you got a name yet? Hey, I know what you should call it. *Pythagoras Pizzeria.*"

"Pythagoras . . . the mathematician?"

"Yeah," said Tab. "He came up with the Pythagorean theorem. It has to do with right-angled triangles."

The trail was flat but we were still walking our bikes. "You guys want to ride?" I asked.

Cheese turned around. "Oh, right," he said. "We're wasting valuable seconds, aren't we?"

The sun went behind a cloud.

"I just thought . . . " I said. "Before the storm comes in . . . "

"Yeah," said Cheese. "It's got nothing to do with you being OCD."

Don't say anything, I thought. *He's just ticked off about the puddle. You'd be mad, too. Just let it slide.*

"What are you boys on about?" said Tab.

"He's got all these lists in his bedroom," said Cheese. "And he's always being, like, a human calculator."

"At least I'm not gifted," I snarled.

"What's wrong with being gifted?"

Tab unclipped her helmet and shook out her hair. "What do you mean, a human calculator?" she asked Cheese.

"He's always counting stuff. Hours, minutes, seconds."

I thought, but didn't say: *You're lucky you're even here. I could've invited anyone to Splitsville. Spencer, Minnow . . . Anyone.*

Instead I said, "I don't like wasting time. We've only got 86,400 seconds in a day. That sounds like a lot, but it isn't."

"And we should care about this because . . . ?" said Tab.

"Because every twelve days you lose over a million seconds of your life. Those seconds aren't coming back. They're gone forever."

Tab looked at Cheese. "This guy's a riot," she said.

Cheese didn't say anything.

Tab slung her helmet over her handlebars. "The jumping rocks aren't far," she said. "If you want to ride on ahead, fill your boots."

I realize now that she was making a sincere offer. But at the time it seemed like she was blowing me off.

"Go ahead," said Cheese. "Time's a wasting."

Was that a smirk on his face? From where I was standing, it was hard to tell.

"That's okay," I said. "If it's only a kilometre, then I'll walk."

Tab turned back to Cheese. "So, tell me more about your restaurant."

"I actually like that name, Pythagoras Pizzeria," said Cheese.

"Sorry, but I've already got it trademarked," said Tab. "But I'd be happy to lend it to you — for a price."

The clouds were really rolling in now. I took one hand off the handlebars and squashed a mosquito on my forehead.

"Everyone will know about Pythagoras after our marketing blitz," said Cheese. "We'll make him more famous than Colonel Sanders."

CHAPTER
11

Panic

Seconds until school: 1,540,000
Until Lights Out: 140,446,000

I've been dreading this part of the story, because it makes me look like a jerk. *More* of a jerk, I mean.

When the trail split in two, we took the path on the left. It was narrow and rocky, and led down a steep hill. Tab suggested we drop the bikes, so we stashed them under some manzanita bushes.

"This way," Tab said.

The trees thinned out. It got bright and I put on my sunglasses. After a minute we came to a lake.

"Almost no one knows it's here," said Tab.

These lakes all looked the same to me, but Cheese started serving up a real crap casserole. He said that the view really "lanced him through the heart," and that it was "more beautiful than the Google homepage" — stuff like that.

"Is this the lake where we found the rowboat?" I asked.

Tab said no. "That's Mislaid Lake," she said. "The cut-off for that's another kilometre up the trail, and on the other side. This is Big Hawk Lake. It's super clean. Take a drink."

Cheese knelt down and slurped water right out of the lake. "Delicious!" he said. "A cascade of glacial refreshment."

We hiked along the shoreline to a bay. Cheese looked up at the rocks and said, "You're kidding . . . you jump from *that*?"

"Of course," said Tab. "And so will you. Come on!"

We walked across a flat sheet of bedrock until we came to a colossal wall of rock. Tab pulled off her shoes.

"Um," said Cheese.

"Oh, come on," said Tab. "It's not as scary as it looks."

Her top changed from blue to white. She must've been wearing her bathing suit underneath.

She started scrambling up the cliff. Suddenly she stopped. "Aren't you coming?" she called down.

"No thanks," Cheese said, sitting down against a boulder. "I enjoy not being a quadriplegic."

Tab let out a *"pfffft."* Then she turned to me. "What's your excuse?" she said.

Yeah, it had to be a one-piece bathing suit. I looked up at the cliff. I couldn't see the top.

"Give me just a second," I said.

"Okay," she said. "But you better not crap out on me."

With that, she turned back to the rock and started climbing.

"Is she at the top yet?" I asked Cheese a minute later.

"Not yet," he said.

"It's high, eh?"

"Uh, yeah."

We said nothing more. *At least we're talking,* I thought.

"Don't worry," Cheese said. "The water looks pretty deep. As long as you jump out a couple of metres, you'll probably be okay."

Probably?

Tab's voice floated down. "Look out below!"

And then a spear of white dropped toward the water. "Ho-ly," Cheese gasped.

I began counting: "One thousand and one, one thous– "
Splash!

She sliced into the water like a pencil.

"Beautiful," said Cheese. "Unbelievable!"

She'd been in free fall for *nearly 2 seconds*. Which meant the cliff had to be . . . Quick calculation . . . 0.5 times the gravitational constant times the square of 1.75 seconds . . . *Doot doot doot* . . . She'd fallen 15 metres.

Fifteen metres. Nearly 5 storeys.

Tab whooped as her head popped out of the water. "Holy macaroni, that was good!" she cried.

She swam back to shore and pulled herself onto the rocks. "Okay, Finn," she said, squeezing water from her hair. "Your turn."

Cheese whispered to me: "Want me to climb ahead? You know, to show you where to grab?"

Ordinarily I would have said yes. But I already felt guilty about cutting him off and making him crash.

"That's okay," I said. "I can do this myself."

"It doesn't look too bad," Cheese said, looking up at the cliff. But he didn't sound all that convinced.

I pulled off my T-shirt and tossed it to the ground.

"Attaboy!" Tab shouted.

"Good luck," Cheese said, in a voice that was hard to read.

I started up the cliff. It was easy at first, since there were lots of handholds and toeholds. And there was a thick rope, too, to pull yourself up. I climbed hand over hand. Rock, rope, pull. Rock, rope, pull.

"You're nearly there," Cheese shouted up. His voice seemed to come from a long way away.

Rock, rope, pull. Rock, rope, pull. I stopped to take a break. The lake looked like a huge turquoise tablecloth stretched out beneath me.

"What's taking him so long?" I heard Tab say.

Keep going, I told myself. *You can do this. You're not scared.*

Finally I got to the top.

"Don't think!" Tab called up. "Just jump! Right now!"

"Yeah," Cheese laughed. "If you stop to think, you'll chicken out."

But it was too late. I'd already looked down toward the water. All I could see was a greenish-blue blur.

"C'mon!" Cheese shouted. "You can do it!"

No, he was wrong. I *couldn't* do it.

I crouched down, knees to chest. I could barely breathe. My heart was hammering like mad.

Take it easy, Finn. Count backwards from twenty.

Twenty . . . nineteen . . . eighteen . . . seventeen . . .

When I got to zero I wasn't feeling any better, so I pressed my finger against the rock and traced the number eight, over and over. *Eight plus eight is sixteen. Sixteen plus sixteen is thirty-two . . .*

"What's the holdup?" Tab shouted.

"Give him a minute," Cheese said. "He may surprise us."

But as hard as I tried, I couldn't stand up. I kept tracing that figure eight over and over.

I looked down toward the lake. I couldn't really see the

water. The trees and rocks and everything else all blurred together. *No way,* I thought. *Nobody can jump from this height. No way could I ever do that and survive.*

Continue to breathe, Finn. Thirteen . . . twelve . . . eleven . . .

I don't know how long I crouched there on the cliff, but the next thing I knew, Tab was kneeling right beside me.

"Take it easy," she said. "None of this matters." She put her hand on my shoulder. "It's just a stupid cliff."

I tried to stand up.

"No pressure," she said. "Take your time."

I pushed myself to my feet, but then I knelt back down. Black dots with fireball tails swam in front of my eyes.

"Come on, Finn!" Cheese shouted. "This is your moment!"

He was wrong. This wasn't my moment. It was — hell.

What was wrong with me? I wasn't afraid of risk. I specialized in risk. I'd just raced down the Organ Donor on a bike.

"*Some of your hobbies will have to change,*" Dr. Zhang had said.

Is *this* what she meant? No more having fun?

Forget that. I crawled to the edge and looked over. *What are you scared of?* I asked myself.

Suddenly I realized: I was scared of the falling. The falling to pieces. The falling away.

Plus, I was scared of not knowing where I'd land.

Ever change your mind fifty times in two seconds?

Okay, I'm doing it. Wait, no I'm not. What am I doing up here? Who do I think I am?

"How are you feeling now?" Tab whispered.

"Not good," I said. "I just . . . I need to get down."

"No big deal," she said. "This isn't for everyone. It's cool."

She took my arm and steered me away from the edge. Then she handed me the rope and I started climbing back down. I made it to the first ledge without any trouble. Wait — someone was climbing up. They needed to pass.

"Excuse me," Cheese said.

I squeezed back against the cliff to let him by. He was wearing his life jacket. "You're not serious," I said.

But he was. He got to the top and said, "Hey, Tab." Then he screamed, "Cowabunga!" and leapt right off.

"Whoa," Tab laughed. "He actually did it!"

One thousand and one. One thous—

SPLASH!

A moment passed. Then I heard sputtering from below. Tab was clapping. "That was *awesome!*" she shouted.

I looked down at the void. He'd actually done it. After saying that it "wasn't his thing."

"It's fun," Cheese shouted up. "Hey, Finn, you've GOT to jump! It's awesome. It feels like jumping from the moon!"

CHAPTER
12

Blur

Seconds until school: 1,537,200
Until Lights Out: 140,443,200

I wanted to punch his doofusy face.

After that first jump, Cheese made two more. After his third, I needed to bolt.

Cheese wasn't supposed to make those jumps. *I* was.

I was the daredevil. He was the dweeb.

I walked along the rocky shoreline. Cheese and Tab didn't notice me going.

Didn't know how to swim. Yeah, right. Cheese had been playing me all along. He just wanted to show off in front of Tab.

I hated myself. My life was nuclear dog crap. I ran up the trail and pulled the bike out from under the bushes.

I needed to get on the trail and just *ride*. That what I always used to do, back when I could see properly. Nothing calmed me down better than a sweaty hour on the trail.

I pushed the bike to the Organ Donor. I figured I'd just go for a little ride. Maybe climb one hill and then turn around. No big deal, right?

Except that it was. It was practically suicidal. But I was so wound up, I didn't care. Tab had said Mislaid Lake was just another kilometre down the trail. Not even a 5-minute ride.

I took out my phone and tapped my GPS pedometer. *Voice activation on*, it trilled.

I climbed onto the bike and pushed off. I rode slowly at first, remembering the hairpin turns and boulders. But it was like when you've got a Starburst in your mouth. You want to suck it slowly to make it last, but it's so delicious, you can't help but chew.

That's how it felt when I got on the bike. I had this overwhelming urge to chew up that trail.

12 kilometres per hour, said the phone.

I cranked the bike forward so hard the frame made cracking noises. *Watch the brown,* I thought. *That's the path. Just keep the bike pointed at the brown.* For a moment my back tire slid sideways in some mud, but I jerked the handlebars to the left, and the rear wheel snapped into line.

I ground my way to the top of the hill. Somehow I didn't feel scared anymore. The panic I'd felt at the top of the jumping rocks was gone.

Going downhill now. Hands squeezing brakes.

8 kilometres per hour, said the phone.

All good.

15 kilometres per hour.

No problem.

17 kilometres per hour.

My eyes were streaming.

19.

The bike hummed beneath me.

21.

Bottom of the hill, heading into another incline. Slowing down, slower, slower.

3 kilometres per hour.

Full stop.

I set one foot on the ground and looked behind me. I'd just ridden down a hill *without a guide.*

Victory is mine!

I pushed off and started pedalling again, only faster. *YES,* I thought, *I'm riding a bike* by myself! It felt so good to be spinning my legs again. My arms were taut but relaxed, ready to absorb the shock waves from the trail. Best of all, my brain was quiet. It wasn't counting the seconds or coming up with new items for my lists . . . or anything.

All too soon, I came to another hill. *I'll just climb this one,* I thought, *and then I'll turn back.*

I dropped down into my granny gear and dug in. This hill was steeper than the first one, and when I got to the top I was deep inside my pain cave.

The downhill was sweet, as always.

13 kilometres per hour.

Smooth sailing.

17 kilometres per hour.

Bring it on!

24.

Um . . .

27.

Houston, we have a problem. The trail suddenly went soft, and the bike started to shudder. I twisted the handlebars to the left, but the back wheel slid away. I leaned into the turn, but it wasn't enough. The bike went end over end.

Eject! Eject!

Whump! Clack! Crack!

I have no idea if I lost consciousness or not. My back was in agony, and the bike was lying on my face.

0 kilometres per hour, said my phone.

I took a few deep breaths and pushed the bike away. I staggered to my feet and unfastened my helmet. It was cracked on one side. Had that crack been there before? No idea.

The Organ Donor strikes again, I thought.

I checked over my body. My left shin was burning. I reached down and felt blood and torn skin.

Great, just great. I picked up the bike. The tires were still inflated — good. My phone was still clipped to my shorts, thank goodness. I dragged the bike back to the trail. Hang on a second. Where *was* the trail?

I looked around. *Crap. Just . . . crap.*

When I crashed, had I fallen to the left? Or to the right? I couldn't remember.

Calm down, Finn. Just calm down.

I remembered something my dad told me once. He said: "Chess games aren't won by smart moves. They're lost by bad ones, made in haste."

I wandered back and forth, hoping to see the trail.

Stay calm, I repeated to myself. *Stay calm. Be cool.*

An airplane rumbled overhead. Clouds of mosquitoes swarmed around me.

I grabbed the bike by the handlebars and pushed it deeper into the forest. Dry twigs cracked under my feet. I thought about that cougar.

Calm down. Don't think about that.

I scouted around for 5 minutes, but couldn't find the trail.

Chess games are lost by bad moves . . .

Checkmate.

And then I saw the blue light.

It was well below me, down a steep slope. It looked like the same light I'd seen three days before, when I'd hiked up here with Cheese.

Yes, I thought. *So it's real after all.* I *hadn't* imagined that blue light. It wasn't a hallucination.

I pushed the bike ahead of me down the slope, but all these prickle bushes kept getting snagged in the crankshaft. Finally I hoisted the bike onto my shoulder. That was better.

If the flashing light is coming from the floating island, I thought, *then Mislaid Lake has to be nearby.* That would mean I wasn't lost after all. I could just wait there until Cheese and Tab came and found me.

And in the meantime, I could take another peek at that island.

Sure enough, a few minutes later I saw a flash of blue between the trees. I walked toward it, the breeze on my face. When I reached the shoreline, the floating island was right there.

Seriously! It was just a few metres offshore. Almost as if it was waiting for me.

I waded into the water; the bike still slung over my shoulder. The water felt nice against my skinned leg. I took ten steps and brushed away the lily pads and bulrushes at the island's edge. There was a dazzling blue glow all along it; a filament of electricity where the water met the earth.

Okay, so it hadn't been just my imagination. This was *real*. Something seriously weird was going on.

I pushed the bike onto the island, and the flashing became brighter. The bike rolled a few metres and then toppled over. I took a deep breath and pressed my hip against the soil. Then I launched myself forward and felt that same stomach-churning drop as the last time.

CHAPTER
13

Serious Cranial Disharmony

Seconds until school: ?
Until Lights Out: ?

First I felt that spine-cracking YANK, and then I was back in
the express elevator, going down.

It was a sickening feeling, like I was falling from a great
height. My whole body tensed up, bracing for impact. My eyes
were all scratchy, as if I'd been swimming for hours in a chlo-
rinated pool.

I tried to breathe deeply, in and out.

The falling ... The falling away ... The falling to pieces ...

Once again I was surrounded by a blue light. Parts of
my body seemed to evaporate as it flashed. My hand would
dematerialize and then, a minute later, it would reappear. I
was used to weird stuff happening with my eyes, but this was
something else.

I kept falling at a zillion kilometres per hour. Finally, after
what seemed like forever, the falling sensation stopped. The blue
strobe light faded, and I pressed my head against the ground.

Eventually I think I slept.

When I woke up, I was lying on my back, staring at a bleached-out sky. I remember thinking: *What's that scar in the sky?* But after a few painful breaths, I thought, *That's no scar. It's a vapour trail from an airplane.*

At the tip of the vapour trail I saw a tiny airplane. Weirdly, it wasn't moving. It was just sitting up there in the sky.

I sat up and rubbed the crust out of my eyes. Then I leaned forward and threw up. I felt better afterwards.

I looked back at the sky. The vapour trail was as crisp as two lines on a highway. *Back up the train,* I thought. *I hadn't hallucinated or had a stroke. This was one hundred per cent real. My vision was back!*

"HA!" I shouted, getting to my feet. "I can *see!*"

It was as if I'd been living in a muddy pond for years, and now I'd finally come up to the surface and flushed the scum from my eyes. I did my touchdown dance, but then I suddenly stopped.

Easy, Finn. You're on a floating island. Chill.

Except that . . . it *wasn't a floating island.* From here it looked more like a spit of land jutting out from the shoreline. Beyond the two trees was that golden cornfield, and past that, the line of purple hills. The floating island only *looked* like an island. But from here, it seemed more like a portal into some goes-on-forever world.

I picked up a stone and tossed it at the lake. It flew through the air and then *BAM* — it suddenly stopped and just floated there in mid-air, like it had smacked into an invisible catcher's mitt.

I reached down to scratch my leg and . . . *Hang on.*

My left shin wasn't bleeding, which was mega-weird, considering how badly I'd sliced it when I'd crashed off the trail.

Add it to the list, I thought. The ever-expanding list of *Things They'd Never Believe Back Home.*

I looked down at the water. Once again the whole lake appeared solid, as if it was sculpted out of metal. A school of minnows sat beneath the surface. They weren't moving. They looked like they were suspended in glass.

I looked back at the shore, just a few metres away. I could see a chipmunk halfway up a tree trunk. It wasn't moving either.

Farther down the bay, I could see the wooden dock and the rowboat — the same one me and Cheese borrowed the last time we were here. The shimmering blue light caught my attention again. It ran all the way along the water line — like some kind of boundary. On this side, you saw one thing. On that side, another.

I grabbed the bike by the handlebars and wheeled it between the two trees. "Anyone home?" I called out. "Free high-fives!"

I pushed the bike through the cornfield. The cornstalks were taller than my head. *Weird, seeing corn out here,* I thought. *I'm high up in the mountains. Corn grows mostly in valleys.*

Add that to the list of *Things I Do Not Know.* How can corn grow at such a high altitude?

As I walked, I came up with more questions. For instance: Why weren't there any bugs out here? Whenever I walked through farmer's fields back home, there were zillions of grasshoppers and aphids and stuff. But here, silence.

It was hard work, pushing the bike down that cornrow. The ground was bumpy, and much too sandy for riding.

Finally I popped out at the far edge of the field. Not far away was a single-track trail. I walked the bike over and swung my leg over the frame. I had eyes that worked, so I was darn well going to use them.

"Up, up and away," I muttered.

I jammed my feet down on the pedals.

CHAPTER
14

Joy Volcano

Seconds until school: ?
Until Lights Out: ?

When I got to the top of the first hill, I stopped to scan the next section of trail. It ran along the top of the ridge for a little way, and then it dropped into a minefield of exposed rocks. Cheese-grater rocks, we called them back home. One fall and you'd be shredded like a hunk of cheddar.

I teetered on the hilltop, thinking things through. *You can do this*, I told myself. *Your eyes work fine here.*

I hovered on the lip, my toes clinging to the ground. I was scared again. Scared my eyes might crap out at any moment.

Oddly, I was more scared now, with eyes that worked, than I'd been back on the Organ Donor when I could barely follow Cheese's shirt. Here, I could see too many terrifying details — rocks, roots, stumps. Skull-crushing boulders.

Don't be scared, I told myself. *Release the brakes. Just go.*
No. That trail is steep!

I wished I had an Allen key to lower my seat post. *Trust your eyes*, I told myself.

Somehow I found the guts to push off. I hadn't even decided which line I was going to take. My brain would figure it out on the fly, right? It would have to.

I picked a line, prayed I could hold it and shoved off.

Look out — fallen tree in 3 . . . 2 . . . 1 . . . Go!

I shifted all of my weight back onto my hips and did a manual, wresting the bike up and over the tree. When my rear wheel landed, I cranked the pedals again. Pushed my speed back up. The chain whispered as it rolled over the sprockets.

BAM! Gap jump. I hung in the air for what felt like 3 seconds. Rough landing — the trail was softer than mashed potatoes. My rear wheel slashed left and right like an angry snake. The tires must've been covered in suction cups, though, because I somehow stayed upright.

Phew — that was sketch. Nearly did some grievous bodily harm there.

If only Tab could see me now.

WHOOPS! Tree stump! Stop daydreaming, Finn.

* * *

There's this word Cheese uses. Proprioception. The lightning-fast communication between your muscles and your eyes.

Example. When you ride your bike, you don't look at the ground beneath your tires. You look farther down the path, where you're going to be in 3 or 4 seconds. Somehow your brain remembers what it sees and delivers that information to your muscles a few seconds later, when it's needed.

Lately, ever since my eyes started to crater, I hadn't been doing much proprioceping.

"Nope," Cheese had agreed. "No proprioception for you. You've got *noprioception*."

Noprioception. That made me laugh. But now I was propriocepting like crazy!

My eyes were scanning 30 metres down the trail, while my muscles were leaning into curves, dealing with the butt-breaking potholes.

WHOA — hanging tree branch. *Duck!*

Close one. Almost got clotheslined there.

Watch it — rock garden!

No time to dodge that one. I just hucked it and hoped for the best.

The bike, I was happy to learn, was actually pretty good. It was heavy but tough. It was more assault vehicle than bike.

At the bottom of the valley, the trail swung left. I carved a turn so sharp my rear tire sent up a rooster tail of dirt.

Then I was riding over a wooden bridge. *Fubbedah! Fubbedah! Fubbedah! Fubbedah!*

Still alive. I'd somehow made it down. My heart was a joy volcano. A joycano.

The trail veered toward another field, so I cut a sharp corner when ... WHOA — living person! I grabbed a mittful of brakes.

* * *

She screamed so loud, I thought my eardrums would pop.

"Sorry," I said, climbing off the bike. "I didn't mean to startle you."

She was kneeling on a straw mat; her eyes were as wide as frying pans. "I can't believe it," she whispered. "You found a way in."

I unclipped my helmet and slung it over the bike seat. "Yeah ... " I said. "I guess I did."

She was older than me. Twenty-five, maybe thirty. She was wearing yellow capris and a lime-green hoodie over a white T-shirt. The T-shirt had a picture of Chewbacca on the front, but I could only see half his face since the hoodie was mostly zipped up.

She was tall, with long arms and legs. A ponytail spilled out the back of her Boston Red Sox ball cap.

"It's just been so long since anyone came," she said.

I lay the bike down on the ground. "Yeah, well, sorry I'm late," I ventured. "Traffic was heavy."

That earned me a smile. She thrust her arm out, as if she wanted to shake hands, but wasn't sure how. I reached forward, turned her hand ninety degrees and we shook.

"I'm Finn," I said.

"Hi, Finn," she said. She had a lopsided smile.

"And you are?" I prompted.

"Oh, yes, that's right. I'm Constant," she said. "Sorry, I've forgotten how to play well with others." She giggled.

Her hand was as dry as a chalkboard. She kept shaking my hand — like she didn't know when to let go.

"I'm sorry I scared you before," I said.

"That's okay," she said. "I'm just glad for the company."

I let go of her hand and she walked back over to the straw mat. She was side-eyeing the heck out of me.

"Did you come here on a Glimmer Line?" she asked.

"Glimmer Line?"

She knelt down on the mat. "You must've seen a flashing light."

"Right," I said. "I did."

The expression on her face kept changing. One second she

had that lopsided smile, and then her forehead would flatten out and her eyes would turn serious.

"Did you have any stomach distress?" she asked.

I nodded. "Total vomitorium."

The skin around her nose crinkled up and she looked as though she was going to laugh. "Don't worry," she said, lying down on her stomach. "You'll get used to that."

She used her arms to raise her head toward the sky. I thought she was going to do a push-up, but instead she held the pose and took a long, deep breath.

"What are you doing?" I asked.

"Cobra pose," she said. "You should try it. Works wonders for the back."

She relaxed her arms and lowered her forehead to the ground.

"Do you live here?" I asked, looking around.

Constant turned her head sideways and smirked. "That's one way of putting it," she said.

She sat up and took off her cap. Her hair was deer-coloured and scraped straight back off her face. Her eyebrows were shaped like little hockey sticks and her eyes were dazzling green. I'd never noticed anyone's eye colour before. But her eyes were as green as new grass.

"Are there any houses here?" I asked, looking around.

Constant angled her head. She seemed confused by the question. "Why ever would you need a house?" she said.

"I don't know," I said. "To sleep in, maybe?"

This caught her off guard. "Why?" she asked. "Are you tired?"

I thought about that for a second and then said, "No."

"Are you hungry? Thirsty?" She looked alarmed.

I shook my head.

"Good," she said. "I used to love eating, but I sure don't miss the cooking or cleaning up."

She still hadn't answered my question about the houses. I looked at the razor scrape of the hilltops against the sky, the birch trees so arrow-straight they could be used for hydro poles.

"Why so happy?" Constant said.

Was I grinning again? "Everything's just so clear," I said. "And there are sharp lines everywhere. I'm not used to it."

"Why not?"

"Because, uh, of my eyes."

Constant leaned forward, stretching out her leg. "What's wrong with your eyes?"

She sat cross-legged on the ground while I talked. When I was done, she looked upset. She stood up and stared at the field.

"Don't worry," I said. "I can see fine here."

"Oh, I'm not worried at all . . . " she said. Then she stopped and turned back around. "I'm sorry, that's not what I meant to say. What I mean is, that's awful about your vision. I'm sorry. I just . . . "

"It's okay," I said, shifting uneasily. I hadn't wanted to discuss my eyesight anyway. "What *is* this place?" I asked. "It's really strange."

Constant smiled sadly. "That's kind of hard to explain," she said. "But tell me more about your Glimmer Line. Where did you see the flashing?"

"On the floating island," I said. "All around the edge."

She squinted as if she didn't believe me. "Islands don't float," she said.

"So people keep telling me."

The wrinkles in her forehead smoothed out. Then she grinned so massively I could see her gums.

"I knew it," she said, putting her cap back on. "I figured there had to be another Glimmer Line around."

I looked up at the purple hills and felt another surge of joy. *I can see*, I thought again. *I can actually see.*

"Is anyone else here?" I asked.

Her facial expression changed again.

"I don't believe so," she said. "I'd know it if they were."

Now she looked confused, as if she was playing a game of Concentration and had forgotten where the matching pairs had all gone.

"This is your first visit here, right?" she asked.

"Second," I said. "But I only stayed for a couple of minutes the first time."

"Freaked you out?"

"Yeah," I said.

She laughed. "It's a weird place, all right. But it's got some nice perks. Especially for someone in your situation."

Just like that, my happy feeling vanished. I went quiet for a minute or two.

"Have you got a bucket list?" Constant asked.

"A what?"

"You know. A list of things you want to see before your vision goes."

I shook my head. I had lots of lists. But I'd never made a list of things I wanted to see.

"Have you ever seen the *Mona Lisa*?" Constant asked.

I shook my head.

"What about the Grand Canyon?"

"No."

Her hair wasn't actually deer-coloured, I noticed. It was lighter than that. It was the colour of perfectly toasted white bread.

"Well, you need to get moving, kiddo," she said. "Five years isn't much. Time's ticking. Well, actually, no, it's not." She barked out a sort of laugh.

Right there. That's the moment someone should have grabbed me by the shoulders and said, "Kid, you can still leave if you want."

"What do you mean?" I asked.

Constant's smile disappeared. "Oh, come on," she said. "You must've noticed."

"Noticed *what*?" I asked.

Constant looked at my shoes, which were still wet from wading through the lake. "You can't have missed the anomalies," she said. "You said your Glimmer Line is on an island, so you must've seen the water . . . "

"It looked like it was frozen," I said.

"Exactly," she said. "But it wasn't. Not really."

Last chance, Finn. Take that bike and go. After this, there's no turning back.

"I don't understand *how* it works," Constant said. "But time operates differently here than it does on the other side."

"What do you mean?"

"Time stretches here."

Turn and run! Go home now. You'll have to apologize to

Cheese and Tab, but it'll be better than this freak show.

Constant was still talking. " . . . time lasts longer here than back home. A second lasts — oh, I don't know — a year. Or ten years . . . Maybe more."

"Is that why the water wasn't moving?"

"That's how it looks to you and me," she said. "But on the other side of the Glimmer Line, it's sloshing around like normal."

I need a time out. I need time to think.

"And people?" I asked. "Do they get frozen, too?"

"Not really. They only look that way from here."

I remembered what Cheese looked like the first time I stepped on the island. I'd thought he was dead. But . . . he was just moving really slowly?

Alert! Alert! Head exploding!

"You could come here for a century," Constant continued, "and then go back, and nobody would even notice you'd been gone."

"So if I went home right now . . . " I said.

"It'd be the exact same moment as when you left."

My brain filled up with crazy thoughts. It was like having a toilet overflow in my head. I could stay here for a weekend, and my parents would never notice. I could hang out here for a year and not miss a single day of school.

That meant . . . Well, I wasn't sure what that meant. Except this: I didn't have 140 million seconds left until Lights Out. I had a million times that many. A *billion* times that many.

Constant watched me closely. "Does that make you happy?" she asked.

I tilted my head at the sky. It was the colour of skim milk.

I couldn't see the sun, which was strange since there weren't any clouds.

"But how is that possible? It doesn't make sense."

Constant shrugged and shoved her hands into her pockets. "If I run into an astrophysicist, I'll be sure to ask about that."

My chest was exploding with triple exclamation marks. It felt like the first day of summer break.

"How long have you been here?" I asked Constant.

She shrugged.

"A year?" I asked.

She adjusted her cap.

"Seriously? Longer than a year?"

She stared off into the distance. I realized then — crazy as this sounds — that she'd been here way longer than a year. Who even knew how long?

"I call this place Perpetuum," she said, kicking the ground. "Because it'll be here forever. In *perpetuity*."

CHAPTER
15

Clockeyed

Seconds until school:

99
x 999
x 999,999
x 999,999,999
x 999,999,999,999
x 999,999,999,999,999
x 999,999,999,999,999,999
x 999,999,999,999,999,999,999
x 999,999,999,999,999,999,999,999
x 999,999,999,999,999,999,999,999,999
x 999,999,999,999,999,999,999,999,999,999
x 999,999,999,999,999,999,999,999,999,999,999
x 999,999,999,999,999,999,999,999,999,999,999,999
x 999,999,999,999,999,999,999,999,999,999,999,999,999
x 999,999,999,999,999,999,999,999,999,999,999,999,999,999
x 999,999,999,999,999,999,999,999,999,999,999,999,999,999,999
x 999,999,999,999,999,999,999,999,999,999,999,999,999,999,999,999
x 999,999,999,999,999,999,999,999,999,999,999,999,999,999,999,999,999
x 999,999,999,999,999,999,999,999,999,999,999,999,999,999,999,999,999,999

et cetera

Imagine a world where time stretches endlessly . . . Where time stretches toward infinity, and then keeps on stretching.

And in that world, you answer only to yourself. There are no demands on your time, and no one to boss you around. You have only one challenge: you must decide how to fill that time.

Will you build a life-size replica of the *Titanic* out of toothpicks?

Master ju-jitsu?

Invent a solution for global warming?

You could do all of those things and still make it home for dinner. And no one would even notice you'd been away.

Constant called it Perpetuum, but I called it heaven. There were no worries, no responsibilities; plus, I had all the time in the world.

Best of all, I had functioning eyes. I asked Constant if I could stay for a while.

"Of course," she said. "Heaven knows I could use the company. But I'm not going to be your babysitter, Finn. I've got lots of projects on the go. You'll need to find some hobbies, too — to keep from getting bored."

No problem. I had lots of special projects. I had a whole list now: *Things I Thought I'd Never Be Able to Do.*

"I want to learn some tricks on my bike," I said. "Like, I'd love to do a tailwhip-backflip."

"What's that?" Constant asked.

"You go off a big jump and crank your bars to the left and then the right. That brings the tail of your bike around. While you're doing that, you're also doing a backflip."

Up went the hockey-stick eyebrows. "That's something you really want to do?"

"It's a pretty advanced manoeuvre," I admitted. "But I guess I could always start with a barspin."

"Perfect," Constant said. "But you'll need some kind of ramp, right?"

"I guess so," I said.

"No problem. You've got plenty of time to kill, kiddo."

* * *

I still don't know how long I was there. It was impossible to tell. The sun never appeared, and my phone didn't work, so I couldn't check the time. But I never went to bed or even got tired. It was just one long, endless day.

I'll admit it: I got homesick for a while. I missed Cheese and Tab, and even my parents. But after I started building the ramp, and practising my jumps, I cheered right up.

I didn't spend all my time on the bike, of course. Whenever my tailbone got sore, I'd go and do something else. That's how I came to build my first trail. I found a shovel and clippers, and I used them to clear the bush and build some berms and booters.

When the trail was finished, Constant came and checked it out. We hiked it from one end to the other. It was a couple of kilometres long.

"What are you going to name it?" Constant asked.

"I'm not sure," I said. "I was thinking of Double-Ply Quilted Toilet Paper."

She looked at me like I'd grown a second nose. "What's that supposed to mean?"

"You know," I said. "It's so scary, people will fill their pants."

"But it's not that scary," said Constant.

This was true. I'd built a gap jump and a couple of tables, but none of the drops was more than a half-metre.

"I'll keep thinking about it," I said. "Maybe First Blood would be better."

We reached the end of the trail and started walking back. "You'll never guess what showed up," Constant said.

"Let me try," I said. "Another book?"

She nodded. *"An Introduction to Basic Spanish."*

"What good is a book on Spanish?" I asked.

"No idea," she said. "But I found it, so there must be a reason. Maybe it's for you. Are you taking Spanish in school?"

I shook my head. Constant was always finding books. In addition to a lot of medical journals, she had a whole library of boring memoirs.

I usually found tools and lumber, so I'd drag them over to build the trails and the ramp. I wanted to build a jump line and a pump track, too, but I figured I should get the basics done first.

"I wish some foam would appear," I said.

Constant's eyes narrowed. "What on earth for?"

"I want to install a foam pit under the big jump. So I won't get hurt when I practise my barspins."

"You don't need a foam pit," Constant said.

"Sure I do," I said. "I'll be crashing a lot. I don't even have any elbow or knee pads."

"You don't need any of that stuff. Trust me."

The way she said it told me that was the end of the conversation.

We arrived back at a row of long wooden tables. They were

covered with stacks of books. "Where do you think all this stuff comes from?" I asked Constant.

"Fairies," she said.

I looked around. "Seriously?"

Constant burst into laughter. "I'm kidding. My latest theory — one of many — is that it comes from somewhere beneath the surface. I haven't seen any trap doors, but I keep my eyes peeled. So should you. The more we can learn about this place, the better."

The tables were lined up at the edge of a rolling green field. Sweet-smelling white flowers were all over the place.

"What's the strangest thing you've ever found here?" I asked.

"The truck," she said.

"You found a truck?"

"Yeah. In a meadow not far from here."

"And it runs?"

"So far."

"But what do you use for gas?" I asked.

"I don't drive it very much," said Constant. "But whenever I need to drive somewhere, a can of gas usually just shows up."

The truck was a wreck. There was a hole in the floor and the windshield had a crack down the middle.

"You think it looks bad now?" said Constant. "You should've seen it when I found it. The battery worked, thank goodness, but I had to rebuild the engine by hand."

"You know how to rebuild an engine?" I asked.

"I do now," she said, holding up a book. "That's the great thing about this place. There's plenty of time to learn new skills."

Speaking of skills, Constant taught me how to drive. That's right; I got to strike another item off the list of *Things I Thought I'd Never Be Able to Do.*

Funny story, though: the first time I slid behind the wheel, I got weirdly emotional and nearly started to cry.

Crazy, eh? Or maybe not. Ever since my near-death experience at Drag River, I'd been dealing with the waterworks pretty regularly.

But in the front seat of that pickup — what was that about?

Back in February, when it finally sank in that I was going blind, I started dreaming about the day when I'd get cured.

I had it all planned out. First I'd buy an SUV and then I'd fill it with video games, downhill skis and a mountain bike. After that, I'd drive south. Down through the States and Mexico and Central America. I wouldn't stop, either. I'd keep going through Brazil, Bolivia, Argentina and Chile. I'd hammer every bike trail and ski resort along the way. When I reached the bottom of the continent, I'd live in a cabin beside the ocean, and play all those video games I'd brought. Maybe a Chilean girl would come over and hang out. Or maybe she'd just want to watch a movie with me. Anything's possible.

Sure, I'd be a geezer by then, but I'd have an amazing tan, and my quads would be huge from all that biking.

That was it: my post-cure plan.

Travel, video games, maybe even a girlfriend.

But the most important part of all was the *driving.* To me, driving meant independence. Not asking anyone for help.

That's why I almost lost it when I slid into the driver's seat. It felt like a little piece of my dream was coming true.

"Are you okay?" Constant asked me.

"Of course," I said. "Keys please."

"Not yet," she said. "I need to teach you a few things first."

She explained a bunch of stuff I already knew, like which pedal was the brake and which one was the accelerator. She even showed me how to work the clutch, as if I was completely clueless.

Finally she taught me how to change lanes. Which was hilarious, since there was only one road in Perpetuum — a dirt track.

"Who taught *you* how to drive?" I demanded.

"Nobody," said Constant. "I don't have a licence."

"Seriously?" I said.

"Lane change — right!" she cried.

I ran through the sequence she'd drilled into my head, starting with a glance at the side- and rear-view mirrors. "Let me get this straight," I said. "You're teaching me to drive. But you don't have a licence?"

"And let me get this straight," she replied. "You're learning to drive. And you're half-blind?"

Well, she had me there. I did my shoulder check, flicked on the turn signal and pretended I was spinning the wheel.

* * *

Eventually she let me start the truck. Total thrill, I'll admit. Even though it could barely do 30.

Some things about driving were annoying. Like backing up. It took forever. First you had to stop, then change gears, check your mirrors, and then you had to twist your head around like that girl in *The Exorcist*. Then you had to drive really slow — *Beep, beep, beep* — while squinting through the grubby back window.

Biking was way easier. On a bike, you didn't need to back up. You just pounded your front brakes, did a nose wheelie and whipped the rear wheel around.

Bike: 1. Truck: 0.

Turning the truck around was even worse; especially on that narrow dirt track. First I had to swing the steering wheel in one direction, and then stop and reverse in the opposite direction. Then I had to stop and throw the stick back into forward. Back and forth, back and forth. They called it the three-point turn, but on that little track it was more like a thirty-point turn.

Bike: 2. Truck: 0.

Driving did have *some* advantages, though. You never had to worry about keeping your balance, for one. And if you wanted to go faster, you just leaned on the gas. You didn't have to bust a gut.

"This is super easy," I told Constant.

"Glad you think so," she said, flipping the page of her book.

Yeah, another book. This one about open-heart surgery. Some of the pictures were pretty gruesome.

"Here comes the Executioner," Constant said, pointing at a huge pothole. I slowed the truck way down.

"Both hands on the wheel," Constant said. "That's it; take it easy."

The pickup shuddered as it plowed through the pothole. It sounded like the transmission was giving birth to a dishwasher.

"We really need to fix this road," I said.

"Never!" said Constant. "I like it like this. It reminds me

of the roads when we were on safari. Hey, have you ever done that? Gone on safari in Africa?"

"No," I said.

"You really must," said Constant. "And soon. Before the elephants go extinct."

My side-view mirror had fallen off again. It was dangling from a wire, clunking against the door.

"The elephants are going *extinct*?" I asked.

"Many kinds are endangered," said Constant. "Haven't you heard? The whole planet's in trouble."

We drove past a meadow full of violets, and the smell flooded through the open windows. It reminded me of home.

"But the elephants can't go extinct while we're here, right?" I asked. "Because time is stopped out there. Am I right?"

Constant stared at the glove compartment and didn't say anything. Her face looked sad. I guess it *was* sad about the elephants.

Suddenly, for the first time in what seemed like ages, I thought about home. Cheese, Tab. Even my parents. It might have had something to do with the violets, but that lonely feeling of homesickness was back.

"Why didn't you ever get a driver's licence?" I asked.

Constant lowered her book onto her lap. "Me and my husband lived downtown," she said. "So we never needed a car."

She had a husband? Why wasn't he here? "Do you guys have any kids?" I asked.

The truck rattled over more uneven ground. "One," she said. "A little girl."

Seriously? She had a kid?

"What's her name?" I asked.

"Rowyn."

Constant's face was as flat as a sheet of paper.

"Why isn't she here?" I asked. "If I had a kid, I'd bring her here. This place is amazing. I bet Rowyn would love it."

Forked lines appeared between Constant's eyebrows. She took her sunglasses out of the glove compartment and put them on. Then she reached back and fastened her seatbelt. "Finn," she said, "do you know where the brake pedal is?"

"Of course," I said.

"Great."

Suddenly Constant reached over and yanked the steering wheel to the right. The pickup lurched off the track and into a thicket of bushes. I screamed and tried to twist the steering wheel back.

"FRAAAAAAAAAAA — "

The trees raced toward us.

"FRAAAAAAAAAAA — "

I clamped down on the brakes. We stopped just in time.

"Are you *crazy*?" I shouted.

Constant's eyes were hidden behind her sunglasses.

"What the heck was *that*?" I cried.

Still nothing. I slammed the stick shift into park.

"You almost got us *killed*!" I shouted.

"Not me," Constant said. "That was you. You need to pay more attention to the road."

I glared through the windshield, furious. I swatted off the ignition. The engine shuddered and then died.

"Driving isn't a part-time job," Constant said. "It's not a time to interview me about my family."

I glared across the seat. What was wrong with her? I was

just making conversation; I didn't really need details about her family.

"Fine," I said. "I accept full responsibility." I left a pause. "But you still could've killed us."

"Not possible." She sighed. "We can't die out here."

What?

What did you just say? I stared at her.

"At least, I'm pretty certain," Constant said.

Her book had smashed against the windshield. She stuffed it into the glove compartment and kicked that shut with her knee.

"I mean, our bodies don't age here," she said. "Haven't you noticed? Your hair hasn't grown a millimetre since you arrived. Nothing ever really changes here. Yes, things show up in the fields, and people like you appear from time to time, but our bodies never get any older. Think about it. How many times have you crashed your bike on that ramp? And yet you've never been injured."

Picture a world . . . Where time stretches endlessly . . . Where a blind kid can drive a truck . . . Where you never die.

Suddenly, something clicked in my head. My brain just decided that it had had more than enough weirdness for one day. *You've built a trail and done some amazing jumps,* my brain said. *You've learned to drive a truck. You've learned a second language. Let's call it a day. That's a wrap.*

"You know, I should probably get going," I said. "My parents must be freaking out."

"They haven't even noticed that you left," Constant said.

Right. I knew that. Still, I had to go. "But there's stuff I need to do back home," I said.

Constant was silent for a moment. Then she shook her head. "You seriously want to go back?" she said. "To *that place*? With its earthquakes and diseases? Its poverty and wars?"

Her outburst confused me; her face confused me even more. It was full of red blotches and worry lines. Was she trying to convince me to stay? How come? Was she lonely?

Her face suddenly shifted gears, and she switched on her high-beam smile again. Only this time, it looked totally fake. "If that's your idea of a good time, then go ahead," she said. "Just don't blame me if you can't get back."

"Huh?" I said. *What was that supposed to mean?*

Constant shrugged. "I don't mean to scare you," she said, "but Glimmer Lines aren't always reliable."

Symptoms of a panic attack:
Increased heart rate
Elevated levels of adrenaline
A desire to run screaming for the hills

"What do you mean, Glimmer Lines aren't always *reliable*?" I asked.

Constant sighed. "Sometimes they work, sometimes they don't. Sometimes they let you bring things in, but even if they do, you can't always take them back out."

Her face looked like a fallen-down barn. It reminded me of my dad's face that day in the car.

I'm sorry, son. I'm so, so sorry.

I grabbed the door handle and flung it open. Where'd I leave the bike? I had to find it — fast.

"Take it easy, kiddo," said Constant. "I bet your Glimmer

Line works fine. I'm just an old worrywart. Pay no attention to me."

The bike is back at the trail. Can I run there from here? I'll find the bike and ride over the purple hills. After that, then what? Through the cornfield. Look for the two trees . . .

"Relax, kiddo," Constant said. "I'm just having a tough day. My studies . . . Well, I thought I might have a lead on something, but it's just a dead end."

I wasn't listening. I was spinning out — like the time I'd freaked out at the top of the jumping rocks.

"Come on," said Constant. "Let's you and me hit the trails. Or I could quiz you on your Spanish. Come on, it'll be fun."

No. I couldn't. I was too busy falling.

Falling to pieces.

With no idea where I'd land.

I climbed out of the truck and looked back at Constant. "Come with me," I said. "You can meet my friends. Have dinner at Splitsville."

She stared at a patch of violets beside the track. "Thanks for the offer, but I've got studying to do."

What was with her mysterious studies?

"Come back, and I'll explain," she said. "Maybe you could help us out."

Us? Who's us?

Constant smiled. Were her eyes shiny? No, it was just a trick of the light.

"I'll be back," I said, slamming the driver's seat door.

"Of course you will."

I turned away from the truck and ran.

CHAPTER
16

Blindsided

Seconds until school: 1,533,900
Until Lights Out: 140,439,900

Thank you, Lord. I made it through.

That was my first thought when I crossed back over the Glimmer Line. My second thought wasn't anywhere near as cheerful: *How can anyone live like this?!*

A moment ago I'd been staring at a chipmunk on a birch tree. I could see the stripes on its back and everything. Now I couldn't see the chipmunk, and the tree was just a blurry white stripe. The mountains once again looked like piles of steamed spinach.

Vision: chopped in half. Confidence: pooched.

Had my eyesight *really* been this bad before I'd gone to Perpetuum? Yeah, okay, I guess it had.

All those sharp lines I'd grown used to in Perpetuum were gone. They'd all bled into each other, like chalk drawings in a rainstorm.

How was I supposed to find my way to the trail? I wanted to drop kick my *Stupid! Useless! Eyeballs!* into the Drag River gorge.

I was standing in a half-metre of water. The island was floating somewhere behind me.

First things first, I thought. *Find your sunglasses.*

I felt around on my head, but they weren't there. Checked my pockets. Not there either.

Okay, fine, I thought. *A Glimmer Line fail, but at least a small one. But . . . where's the bike?*

I waded back and forth through the shallows. Five seconds ago it had been resting on my shoulder. Now it was vaporized. Just . . . poof.

Finally I gave up looking and staggered to shore. I slumped down on the bank.

At least my phone had made it through. That was the only bit of good news I could find. Constant was right, the Glimmer Lines were unreliable. My left shin was itching. I tried to think.

Somewhere behind me, a tree branch snapped.

What was that? An animal? A cougar? Or just the wind?

Crap, I thought. *Why'd I decide to come back?* My eyes were just about useless here.

I splashed water on my face and pushed myself to my feet. I had to get back up to the Organ Donor. It was somewhere above the lake, so as long as I kept going up, I'd have to cross it eventually. Right?

I began to climb. Up, up, up. Smash into tree. Keep going up.

Eventually the ground levelled out and yellow light spread through the forest. Hey — the sun! It had been a long time since I'd seen it. I sat down on a boulder to catch my breath.

Maybe ten minutes passed. Fifteen.

The sun went behind a cloud. I started to shiver.

Pop quiz: Do you know the recipe for disaster?

I do. It looks like this:

Recipe for Disaster:
1. Enter a forest
2. Go alone
3. Make sure the forest is inhabited by cougars
4. Get totally lost
5. Tire yourself out
6. Have a panic attack
7. For best results, follow the above steps while blind

Eventually I heard a faraway echo: "Hey, Finn! Yo, Finn-bot."

It took a second, but I recognized the voice. It was Cheese. He was higher up, on the ridge.

"Down here!" I shouted. "I'm down here!"

The yelling stopped. I stood still and waited. I slapped the back of my neck. Man, these bugs.

The voice sounded again. "Yo, Finn!"

"Here!" I flapped my arms up and down.

Soon he appeared. He was wearing a mud-splattered T-shirt. Tab had on a blue top and capris.

I wanted to hug them both.

"There you are, my good man!" Cheese called out. "Thank goodness; my dendrites have been yearning for your company."

"Dendrites?" said Tab.

"Brain cells, if you prefer." They stopped right in front of me. "Whoa, Finn, what'd you do?"

"What do you mean?" I asked.

"What happened to your leg?" said Tab.

I reached down. My left shin was wet and sticky. That was weird. I hadn't done anything to —

"You're totally gushing blood," said Cheese.

"Bike crash?" Tab asked.

"Uh. It's nothing," I said.

I ran my hand up and down my shin. It felt disgusting — like a chew toy for zombies. I hadn't had any cuts or scrapes in Perpetuum . . . Wait, was this really from that spill I'd taken on the Organ Donor — *before* I left?

Tab pulled a wad of tissues out of her pocket.

"Thanks," I said. "What're you guys doing out here anyway?"

"Nothing special," said Tab. "Just, you know, *saving your life.*"

She was standing right beside me. *Deep breath, Batman.*

"I don't need saving," I said.

"Yeah, right," Tab said.

This was what I'd come back for. *This.*

"I know about your eyes," she said. "You could've got lost out here and died. This isn't a playground."

I turned and looked at Cheese. "You promised you wouldn't *tell*," I growled.

"He didn't tell me anything," Tab said. "I figured it out on my own. It wasn't hard."

The tissues had turned bright red from the blood. I stuffed them into my pocket. Tab gave me some more.

"He's not completely blind," Cheese said. "He's still got half his vision or something."

"Great," said Tab. "So you'll only fall off half of the cliffs. That really puts my mind at ease."

"Stop," I said. "Stop talking. Please."

Tab ignored this. "Sorry, pal, but I'm not letting you die on my watch. Half your vision is a lousy percentage."

Cheese punched my shoulder. "Hey, bud. You okay?"

I bristled. I wasn't ready to be buddy-buddy just yet.

"Why'd you ditch us before?" he asked. "We were having an awesome time."

Oh right — the jumping rocks.

"Hey," I said, "how long has it been since you saw me?"

Cheese seemed surprised by the question. "I don't know," he muttered. "Maybe an hour?"

Seriously? An hour? But I'd learned how to drive. I'd built a whole bike trail. I'd learned so much.

"Where's my brother's bike?" Tab asked.

"Oh . . . not far," I said. "It's down at the lake . . . somewhere."

Cheese made a clicking noise with his tongue. "Did you, uh . . . Did you see the floating island?"

"Yeah," I said. "I landed on it, too."

"Seriously?" he said. "What happened?"

An airplane rumbled through the sky. "What's a floating island?" Tab asked.

She stared at me so long I had to look away.

"If you don't tell me," she said, "I'll flip a table, I swear."

Cheese glanced around. "We're in a forest," he said. "No tables."

"Then I'll lash a bunch of logs together and *build* one," she said. "And then I'll flip it on your pointy heads."

* * *

So I told. I told Tab and Cheese about my time there — at least, the basics. I was glad I couldn't really see the expressions on their faces, especially when the story got more and more weird.

"Just for the record," Cheese told Tab, "Finn saw you from the island the other day. Which is highly irregular in light of his, uh, visual impairment."

Tab snorted.

"I'm serious," said Cheese. "You were half a kilometre away at the time. Either he's got some incredible sort of hot-babe radar, or something totally weird is going on."

"It happened again today," I said. "The moment I stepped onto the island — across the Glimmer Line — I had perfect vision."

"About this thing you call a Glimmer Line," Cheese said.

"It's a doorway," I said. "A portal into Perpetuum."

Tab coughed.

"It reminds me of that movie, *Focus Horizon*," said Cheese. "The one with that actor, the dude who squints . . . "

"Maximillian Forrester?" said Tab.

"Yeah," I said. "Guy spends the whole movie squinting."

"They're digging that tunnel under the ocean," said Cheese. "Trying to patch a leaky oil well. But they hit a vent that leads down to the Earth's core. Something ruptures, and the neutrality is unleashed."

"What's a neutrality?" said Tab.

"I think it's just fictional," said Cheese. "But in the movie, it's a localized zone where time doesn't operate like it should."

"Just like Perpetuum," I said.

Tab shook out her hair and swatted some bugs. Was she grinning? I thought so, but I couldn't tell for sure.

Uh, oh, I thought. *I'm losing her.*

Somewhere below us, at the bottom of the hill, water was lapping against the shore.

"Hey, Tab," I said. "You speak Spanish, right?"

"Portuguese," she said.

"Really? Portuguese?" I said.

"Yeah. How come?"

Crap. I could've sworn she spoke Spanish. Hadn't she said *buenas noches* when she paddled past our dock?

"The two languages have a lot in common, though," she said. "And I can speak a little Spanish."

"Seriously?" I said. *"Me llamo Finn."*

"Mucho gusto," she said. *"¿De dónde eres?"*

Yes! I thought. *All those lessons weren't for nothing.*

"Soy de Edmonton," I said.

"Omigod!" she cried. *"¿Dime qué tal la familia? ¿Cómo están todos?"*

"Muy bien," I said. *"Mis padres vienen de visita este verano."*

I was pretty sure I got that last sentence wrong, but I didn't know how to fix it, and Tab didn't seem to notice.

"When'd you learn to speak Spanish?" Cheese demanded.

"In Perpetuum," I said. "Constant taught me."

"¿Tienes hermanos o hermanas?" Tab asked. Electricity in her voice now.

"No bien."

Cheese grabbed my shoulders and shook me. "You speak Spanish? No WAY!"

He turned to Tab. "This is new," he said. "You have to believe me. Our boy here couldn't speak Spanish this morning."

Tab stared at me.

"I can prove it," I said. "Come to Perpetuum. The floating island is just down the hill."

"Yes!" said Cheese. "Let's check it out."

That's when it happened. Tab reached out and took my hand. High voltage shot through my veins.

"You know this is the craziest thing I've ever heard, right?" she said.

She was staring right at me. Man, her eyes. Freaked. Me. OUT.

"How do I know you won't ditch us?" she said.

Ditch you? I'd never . . . Oh wait. Yes I had.

"I'm sorry I was a jerk before," I stammered. "It's just that . . . I get these panic attacks sometimes."

There. I'd said it. Tab kept holding my hand.

"Plus, I was embarrassed," I said. "Back at the rocks. I'm not normally scared of heights like that."

Her hand was warm and I could smell her breath. Peppermint and pine trees and something else — strawberries?

"That's okay," she said. "But you should've told me about your eyes. I feel like a bad girl scout for dragging you there."

"That's why he didn't want to tell you," said Cheese. "He hates it when people treat him differently."

Tab looked at me. "So when we were on top of the jumping rocks, could you even *see* the water?"

"Not really," I said. "It was sort of a blur."

"You didn't know where you were jumping?"

"Not really," I said.

She let go of my hand and swept her hair off her face. The wind riffled through the trees. *"¿Qué te hizo querer aprender Español?"* she said.

"What does that mean?" Cheese asked.

I knew, but I wasn't about to tell Cheese. *Silly boy*, it meant. *Why'd you go to the trouble of learning Spanish?*

Tab moved a half-step closer. I hoped my eyes were meeting hers.

"*¿Qué te hizo querer aprender Español?*" she repeated.

I said the first thing that came to mind. I wasn't trying to act smooth. It just came out.

"*Tú,*" I said.

I did it for you.

CHAPTER 17

The Landing Party

Seconds until school: 1,531,800
Until Lights Out: 140,437,800

When we got to the lake, the island had disappeared.

After looking across the lake for a minute, Cheese said, "I can see it. Over by that point."

I turned sideways and caught sight of it — *sort of.* I wouldn't have seen it at all if not for the blue light. It was flashing away as usual. Tab could see the island fine, but not the flashing.

"You're telling me that thing is *floating*?" she said.

I nodded. "That's exactly what I'm telling you."

She shielded her eyes with the back of her hand. "But it's so small," she said. "There sure aren't any cornfields."

"It looks totally different once you get onto it," I said. "Like I told you, it's a portal. You'll have to see it to believe it."

She stared at me and then looked back at the lake. A loon called out twice. "Whoa," she said suddenly. "The island just moved."

"Freaky, eh?" Cheese said. "It's like watching a traffic light change from green to yellow, and then to — I don't know — *purple*."

She kept staring over the water. "That is some next-level weirdness," she said.

"We can take the rowboat out to see it," I said. I'd seen it from Perpetuum, when my eyes worked better.

We scrambled along the shoreline, toward the dock, pushing branches away from our faces.

"Hey, Finn." Tab shoved aside more branches. "You said my brother's bike was down here somewhere, didn't you?"

"That's right," I said. "Keep your eyes peeled."

She held back a pine branch so it wouldn't swat my face. "It may be a beater," she said, "but he's been talking about stripping it down for parts."

That was a relief — I could handle paying Tab's brother back a hundred bucks or so, but I was still hoping the bike would turn up.

"Oh, crap." Cheese suddenly stopped walking. "I left my life jacket back at the jumping rocks."

Tab swung an arm around his shoulder. "Don't worry, son," she said. "I'll save you if you start to drown."

Uh, oh. Not good. I needed Cheese to see Perpetuum. Hopefully Tab could convince him to get in the rowboat anyway.

"You guys are going to love Constant," I said. "She's probably the smartest person I've ever met."

"Oh, yeah?" said Tab. "How smart is she?"

"She taught me woodworking and how to drive standard."

"I'm sorry — *what*?" said Tab. "She taught you how to *drive*? Like, *a car*?"

"Pickup truck, actually." I guess I hadn't mentioned that before.

I thought I'd convinced her with the whole speaking Spanish thing, but now I was starting to wonder. I just had to get her to Perpetuum. Then she'd understand. Cheese, too.

"I'm hoping she'll give me some guitar lessons when I go back," I added.

"You play guitar?" said Tab.

I shrugged. "I'm just a beginner," I said. "Unlike him."

"WHAT?" Tab grabbed the back of Cheese's T-shirt. "You didn't tell me you play guitar."

"Captain's Log," said Cheese. "We've got an awkward situation. Prepare to go to hyperspace."

"He writes all his own music," I told Tab.

"Get out!" Tab squealed.

Cheese shrugged. "You wouldn't like it," he said. "It's hyper-aggressive. I like music that's a challenge."

"And you?" Tab said to me. "What kind of stuff do you play?"

"I just noodle around," I said. "Right now I'm trying to learn 'Between the Bones.'"

Tab laughed. "Seriously? MPSQ?"

"Yeah, why?"

"No reason. They're just so . . . so mellow."

"I don't wear black eyeliner or anything. I just like the song."

"Me, too," said Tab.

We got to the dock. The rowboat was where we'd left it. Only now it was half-full of water.

There was a bailer in the boat, so we took turns scooping out water. Then Cheese untied the bowline while I managed to slide the oars into the oarlocks. Cheese sat in the bow, which made me happy because it meant I got to row and face backwards . . . and I got to look straight at Tab.

"It's like rowing a bathtub, eh?" said Tab.

The paddle blades kept skipping across the water. Tab's legs were pretty brown stripes. I did my best not to stare.

"The canoe's a lot faster and easier," I said.

"We've got a canoe at my place," said Tab. "We should portage it up here next time, so we don't have to take the rowboat without permission."

Beads of sweat slid down my back.

Suddenly Tab sat up straight. "What's that?" she said.

"What's *what*?" said Cheese, spinning around.

"*That*." She pointed at one o'clock.

"Weird," Cheese muttered.

I couldn't see anything. "Are we heading for rocks or something?" I asked.

"No," said Tab. "There's a weird line in the water."

"It's alive, whatever it is," said Cheese.

Tab stood up and held out her phone. Then she said. "Oh, it's just a chipmunk."

"I didn't know chipmunks can swim," said Cheese.

"That one does."

I kept on rowing.

"You're totally right," said Cheese. "It *is* a chipmunk."

"Told you."

We drew alongside. I looked over the side of the boat, but saw nothing.

"It's pretty cute," said Cheese.

"It's ratty looking," said Tab. "Looks like a homeless chipmunk. Hey, homeless chipmunk!"

She took some pictures and then passed me her phone. The chipmunk looked scrawny and waterlogged. It had a clump of grass in its mouth.

"It's heading toward the island," said Cheese.

I spun my head and saw the glimmering blue light — 20 metres or so off the starboard bow.

"We're stressing him out," said Tab. "Backpaddle, Finn."

"What'll happen if it lands on the island?" Cheese asked.

"Who knows?" I said.

"He's swimming into the lily pads," said Cheese.

The blue flashing got brighter.

"Whoa!" said Cheese.

"What just happened?" I asked.

"He did a complete one-eighty," said Tab.

"Serious vote of non-confidence," said Cheese. "That little dude did *not* like that island."

Tab leaned over the side and dabbled her hand in the water. "Maybe the island gives off an electrical charge," she said. "One that only animals can sense."

"That would explain the lack of animals in Perpetuum," I said.

"Seriously?" said Cheese. "No animals at all?"

"Not that I saw. Well, except me and Constant, if you want to be exact. There weren't any bugs either."

"No bugs?" said Tab. "Awesome. Let's go."

I yanked on the oar, pivoting the rowboat. A breeze came up, and the island slipped away.

"Where's the chipmunk now?" I asked.

"Heading back to shore," said Tab. "Come on, let's do this."

I pulled hard on the oars to get up some speed.

"More to the left," Cheese said. "A little more. Okay, we're coming into the lily pads."

I rested the oar blades on the transom. We drifted through the reeds. The island shimmered in the sun.

"It still looks like an island to me," said Tab. "It's weird that it floats, but I still don't see any cornfield or mountains."

"Trust me," I said. "When you step across the Glimmer Line, you'll see."

"Doubtful," said Tab. "Who's going first?"

"We should probably go together," I said.

"Bad idea," said Cheese. "I bet the island won't hold your combined weight."

Tab looked at Cheese. "Aren't you coming?" she asked.

"Without a life jacket? No chance."

Tab and I looked at each other.

"Whoever goes first should tie a rope around their waist," Cheese said.

"Why?" Tab asked.

"In case you fall through," he said.

"You don't need to worry about that," I said. "It's totally solid on — Oh, never mind. You'll see."

Cheese untied the bowline and cinched it around Tab's waist.

"Too tight," she said.

"That better?"

"Yeah." She clambered forward and sat on the prow, dangling her feet above the island. The sun went behind a cloud.

"Don't be surprised if weird stuff happens," I said. "Like, if the lake freezes up, or the sky turns yellow."

Cheese laughed. "And if you see any rainbow-coloured

unicorns, don't worry. That's completely normal, too."

Tab giggled. She laughed at everything Cheese said. She lowered herself down and let go of the boat. I waited for the loud CRACK.

It never happened. Tab stood up and turned around. "Anything happening?" she asked.

Cheese checked the time on his phone. "As expected, time continues to pass," he said.

Crap, I thought. *It's not working.* Cheese fed out extra rope as Tab walked.

"The ground is really soft," Tab said. "It's like walking on a slice of soggy pizza."

She walked over to the two trees.

"Can you see the cornfield?" I asked.

"No."

Crap, crap, crap. What's wrong?

"I'm coming back," Tab said.

A few moments later she climbed into the boat. "It's actually pretty cool," she said. "Feels like you're walking on a waterbed or something."

She untied the rope and handed it to me. She didn't say *I told you so* or anything like that.

"Something's not right," I said. "Let me check it out. Hang on, take my phone."

I didn't want to take it to Perpetuum, in case it didn't get back out this time. So I gave it to Cheese and climbed to the bow. That filament of blue light was still glowing along the edge of the island.

"You seriously can't see that blue light?" I asked Cheese and Tab.

They craned their necks to look but said nothing.

"It's bright blue," I said. "Right there."

No response.

I swung my butt onto the prow and then lowered my right leg onto what I hoped was solid ground. The moment I touched down —

CRACK!

I didn't just hear it; I felt it, too.

The burning eyes. The loss of gravity. The gut-twist in my solar plexus.

Down I fell, through the floor of the world. I curled my body into a pebble and closed my eyes.

CHAPTER
18

World's Okayest Mom

Centuries until school:
99
x 999
x 999,999
x 999,999,999
x 999,999,999,999
x 999,999,999,999,999
x 999,999,999,999,999,999
x 999,999,999,999,999,999,999
x 999,999,999,999,999,999,999,999
x 999,999,999,999,999,999,999,999,999
x 999,999,999,999,999,999,999,999,999,999
x 999,999,999,999,999,999,999,999,999,999,999
x 999,999,999,999,999,999,999,999,999,999,999,999
x 999,999,999,999,999,999,999,999,999,999,999,999,999
x 999,999,999,999,999,999,999,999,999,999,999,999,999,999
x 999,999,999,999,999,999,999,999,999,999,999,999,999,999,999
x 999,999,999,999,999,999,999,999,999,999,999,999,999,999,999,999
x 999,999,999,999,999,999,999,999,999,999,999,999,999,999,999,999,999
x 999,999,999,999,999,999,999,999,999,999,999,999,999,999,999,999,999,999
x 999,999,999,999,999,999,999,999,999,999,999,999,999,999,999,999,999,999,999

et cetera

The next thing I knew, I was lying on my back. I rolled onto my side and looked at the rowboat.

Great, just great, I thought.

Tab's hair glistened like polished brass. Cheese's eyes were dull, like old marbles.

They were both frozen solid. Except, they weren't. They were just on the other side of the Glimmer Line — where time actually moved.

And wait a sec. *Ho-ly.*

It was the first time I'd seen Tab up close. I mean, clearly, with eyes that *actually worked.*

What was it Cheese had said?

She had an oval face with well-structured features. A slightly turned-up nose, which wasn't an impediment.

Who was he kidding?

That girl was gorgeous. Her face could melt magazine covers.

I stared at her for a few seconds, and then I thought, *Well crap. What am I supposed to do now?* I'd really wanted to show them Perpetuum. I'd have given anything to see their faces when I did a tailwhip on the bike, or when I rolled up in the pickup truck.

I looked over at the cornfield and then turned back toward Cheese and Tab. Should I stay or should I go?

I'd promised Tab I wouldn't ditch her and Cheese again, but I hadn't counted on them not getting through. Why had the Glimmer Line only worked for me?

I looked at the cornfield, and then back at Cheese and Tab. I must've changed my mind fifty times in twelve seconds.

I picked up a rock and flung it at the lake. The moment it crossed the Glimmer Line, it shuddered to a stop.

I stared at the rock, floating in mid-air. Seeing that would *never* get old.

Still scanning the ground, I pushed myself to my feet. Where the heck had the Snakebite gone?

Finally I made up my mind. I decided to take a quick trip to visit Constant and find the bike. Of course, I'd have to walk the whole way. Not that it mattered. It wasn't like Cheese and Tab would be getting impatient.

* * *

Constant had been busy while I was gone.

She'd built a boardwalk and a corn maze and a two-storey tree house. As well, there were dozens of new bike trails. And a huge octagonal sandbox.

"Constant!" I shouted. "Yo, Constant!"

I followed the dirt track all the way to the Executioner, and then I turned around and walked back. I hiked all around Perpetuum, calling Constant's name. Finally I saw something. "Hey," I muttered. "What are *you* doing here?"

A picnic table sat at the edge of a grassy field. Beneath it, I found the Snakebite.

How did it get way out here?

I picked the bike up by the seat and spun the wheels.

"That doesn't belong to you," said a voice.

I turned around. Recognized the baseball cap. *Yes.*

"Heyo! Comrade Constant!" I said. "W'sup?"

She was wearing plaid pants with matching rips in the knees, and a T-shirt that said *World's Okayest Mom* across the front.

"State your name," she said, folding her arms across her chest.

"I'm Finn," I said. "You taught me to drive — remember?"

She looked exactly the same — except for the new clothes.

"Did you come here on a Glimmer Line?" she demanded.

Seriously? Am I being pranked?

"I already told you all that stuff," I said. "My Glimmer Line is on the floating island. Don't you remember?"

"Islands don't — oh, wait. Wait a second."

Constant closed her eyes and I could see her lips moving. She almost looked as though she was praying.

I shifted back and forth on my feet. Finally she opened her eyes. "You're going blind, right?"

"Bingo," I said.

"Right. I remember now. You're Finn." She walked over and pulled me into a sideways hug.

"Where did you find my bike?" I asked.

"Back at your Glimmer Line," she said. "It must've spat the bike back out when you crossed over. I told you the Glimmer Lines were unreliable, right?"

"Yeah," I said. "But my phone got out."

"Sometimes it works, sometimes it doesn't."

Constant flashed her high-beam smile. "It's great to have you back, kiddo," she said. "I've been going a bit stir-crazy all alone."

"Isn't anyone else here?" I asked.

Constant scratched her neck. I counted the letters on her shirt.

"A woman was here for a while," Constant said. "She helped me build that tree house, I think."

I looked up at the tree house and then back at Constant. "Where is she now?" I asked.

A look of disappointment crossed Constant's face. "She went back through her Glimmer Line, I expect. I guess she got bored here. Some people do."

She wandered over to the picnic table. It was covered with dog-eared books and magazines.

"Did she use my Glimmer Line?" I asked. "Or did she get here on her own?"

"Oh, she had her own, of course. Nice lady, but high strung. Hey, that reminds me. I've got something for you."

She walked over to the tree house, climbed up the ladder and disappeared inside. A moment later she climbed back down with a guitar slung over her back.

"What's *that*?" I asked.

"What does it look like?" said Constant. She unclipped the strap and held it out.

I leaned the bike against a tree and took the guitar. "Oh, wow," I said.

"Like it?" she asked.

I ran my hand over the wood finish. "Where'd you get this?"

"That lady brought it. She tried to take it home, but it didn't get through."

It was an acoustic cutaway with nylon strings. It looked a lot like the Stratocaster that Nathan plays on most of MPSQ's songs.

"You play, right?" said Constant.

I nodded and slung the strap around my neck. *How did "Between the Bones" go again? Oh, right — there it is.*

I played a few bars, but then I got self-conscious.

"Keep going, Finn," said Constant. "Play the whole song. I

haven't heard any music since that woman left."

I tried a few times, but I kept botching up the chorus. Constant didn't recognize the song.

"What were they playing on the radio when you came here?" I asked.

"I never listened much to radio," Constant said. "I sure didn't know the names of many songs."

"What month did you come here? What was the weather like?"

"It was hot — so it must have been summer. There was a big hurricane in Mexico, so it was probably August or September. I was preoccupied at the time, but I remember that hurricane."

"A hurricane just hit Mexico yesterday," I said. "We heard about it on the news."

Constant squinted at an invisible line above the trees. "There was talk of it coming up the coast," she said. "People were stocking up on water and extra batteries."

I hadn't heard about that. "You live near the coast?" I said.

She shook her head. "No, Johnstown's in upstate New York. Pretty far inland. It's gorgeous; you'd love it."

I thought about this. "So where's your Glimmer Line?"

Constant walked over to the bike and squeezed the brake handles. "Where's my Glimmer Line *here*? Or where is it *there*?"

What a weird conversation, I thought. "Where's your Glimmer Line *there*?" I said.

Constant smiled. "You'll laugh," she said.

"No I won't."

She kicked one of the pedals, making the crankshaft spin. "There's a little park right near the hospital," she said.

"And in that park, there's a playground. One afternoon I was swinging on a swing, thinking my own thoughts, when I noticed something flashing between the trees."

"Glimmer Line," I said.

Constant nodded. "Exactly. But at first I thought someone had just dropped a bike light or something. So I wandered over. There was a little gate behind the row of trees, and the whole gate was flashing bright blue. The gate led into an alley that went back up to the hospital, so I unlatched the gate and walked through. Of course, the next thing I knew, it felt like I'd been flushed down a toilet, and then I was suddenly here."

I looked at one of the books on the picnic table. Something about statins and acute coronary symptoms.

Constant followed my gaze and I saw a shiver go through her. I thought she was going to continue her story, but she didn't. "Did you bring your friends with you?" she asked.

"I tried to," I said. "Tab, anyway. But she didn't make it through."

"Oh," said Constant, her grin fading away. "I thought that might happen."

"Seriously?" I said.

"It's just a theory," she said. "But Glimmer Lines only seem to work for one. One person in, one person out."

I wish you'd told me that before, I thought. *I might not have made such a fool of myself with Tab.*

"Tab — that pretty girl you mentioned," Constant said. "Is she the one you learned Spanish for?"

"Yeah," I said. "But I screwed it up. It turns out she speaks Portuguese, and only a little Spanish."

Constant laughed. "Did she understand anything you said?"

"Pretty much everything." I laughed. "Still, I felt pretty dumb."

She smirked and took a quarter out of her pocket. "Did you tell her about this place?"

"Yeah," I said. "But it didn't go over all that well."

Constant nodded and tossed the quarter in the air. She caught it a second later and closed her fist. "It's probably a good thing that she couldn't get through," she said.

"How come?" I asked.

"This isn't the best place to bring a date."

"It wasn't a date," I said. "Tab and I have only known each other a couple of days."

"Mmmm."

Constant opened her fist. The quarter had turned into a stuffed bunny.

"Whoa," I said.

"Guess what I learned since you were here last?" Constant said.

"Survey says . . . magic?"

"Bingo."

She closed her fist around the bunny, and when she opened her hand again, it had turned into a baseball card.

"Impressive," I said

"Not really," said Constant. "Magic is just tricks. If you practise enough, then you're magic."

"If you have enough time, in other words," I said.

Constant shrugged. I picked up the baseball card. Pedro Martinez, Boston Red Sox, 2004.

"What were you thinking about?" I asked. "That afternoon in the park when you found the flashing gate?"

For an instant, Constant looked like she'd swallowed a pill the wrong way. Then her face softened and she produced a smile. "I was hiding from my daughter," she said.

"Rowyn?" I said.

"Yes." She pulled down the brim of her cap. "One day she was complaining about her arm. She said it felt numb, so I took her to see the doctor."

I'd been tuning the guitar, but now I stopped.

"At first we thought she had multiple sclerosis," Constant said. "But she didn't. Turned out she has something worse."

I sat there, holding the guitar, not knowing what to say. What are you supposed to say when someone tells you that? I'm sorry?

"Three days later they were wheeling her into the operating room. It was the worst moment of my life. I honestly felt like I was dying, Finn. I mean, she's only six. Six-year-olds shouldn't have heart problems, right?"

Constant's daughter had heart *problems? But Constant seems so calm, so under control . . .*

"I didn't want Rowyn to see me so upset before her operation," Constant said. "So I walked down the street to that little park. I just needed to have a good cry, you know? So I was sitting and crying on that swing and then I saw that glowing gate . . . "

She closed her eyes, her hands still clutching the stuffed bunny. Wait a second — hadn't she turned the bunny into a baseball card?

"When I woke up," Constant went on, "I was lying in a meadow. I started screaming and running around. I was totally terrified. I was probably here for a grand total of ten seconds — well, in normal time. Then I saw a blue line between the grasses. I jumped across it and *zing*, I was right back in that little park, beside that gate.

"And then?" I asked.

"Well, I raced back to the hospital. I sat in the waiting room for fourteen hours straight. The doctors cut Rowyn's . . . Oh, sorry — sorry."

The skin on her cheek tensed up. Her eyes looked puffy, but she wasn't crying.

Did I say that Constant was about twenty-five? She suddenly looked older.

"Hey," I said, setting the guitar down. "Show me another trick."

She looked relieved. "All right," she said. She slipped the Pedro Martinez baseball card into one of the books on the picnic table. "Okay," she said. "Where's Pedro now?"

I pointed at the book that I knew held the card. She opened it up. Flipped through the pages. Pedro wasn't there.

This happened over and over. I had no idea how she did it. I was looking at the books and she never touched the card, yet the Pedro card kept jumping from one hardcover to another.

Near the end of the trick, Constant told me to rip the baseball card into quarters. I did that, and a moment later it appeared in my back pocket, untorn.

"How'd that get in there?" I demanded.

Constant made a *how-am-I-supposed-to-know* face.

I started to laugh. "That was seriously impressive," I said. "You have to teach me how to do that."

Constant grinned like a biker catching air. Then her smile

faded away. "Rowyn has a rare condition," she said. "There hasn't been much research on it yet. The doctors say it'll only get worse with time. So I thought, if I could do some research — given that I have all the time here I want — I could learn something about Rowyn's disease. Maybe I could help her in some way."

So that explained the medical books and journals.

"Good idea," I said.

"You'd think so," said Constant. "Only, I overstayed my welcome."

I stared at her. What did that mean?

"The last time I tried to go back," she explained, "I couldn't find the blue light. I walked over the spot where it should've been, but there was nothing. No flashing light. No gate. I searched the meadow again and again. Nothing."

"So that means . . . " I said.

"Exactly," she said. "I'm trapped."

"You could use my Glimmer Line," I said. "If you want to go back and see your husband and daughter."

Constant shook her head. "Don't tempt me."

What was that supposed to mean?

"I wouldn't trust myself," she said.

"What do you mean?" I asked.

"I wouldn't trust myself to come back."

What?

"Does that surprise you?" Constant said. "It shouldn't. Never underestimate a mother's love for her kid."

We stood in silence. I felt like I'd swallowed a brick.

"Come on," she said finally. "That's enough of our sad stories. Let's go do something fun."

CHAPTER 19

Return to Splitsville

Seconds until school: 1,530,900
Until Lights Out: 140,436,900

Once again, the return trip was easier. The moment I stepped over the Glimmer Line, there was a soft *fffft* sound, like air being let out of a bike tire. Then I was back in the rowboat with Cheese and Tab, and the mountain breeze was riffling through my hair.

"Did you see that splash?" Tab was saying.

"Probably a turtle coming up for air," said Cheese.

I blinked my eyes. The world was blurry again. Cheese and Tab were still sitting in the middle of the boat.

"That wasn't any turtle," said Tab. "Sounded like someone threw a rock at us."

"Who could've thrown a rock?" said Cheese. "We're in the middle of the lake."

"Hey, guys," I said.

They looked around.

"If you're going to go, then hurry up and go," said Cheese.

Tab draped her arm over the side of the boat and swished her hand through the water. "That is really cold," she said.

"Hey, no splashing!" cried Cheese.

"But the water's so refreshing," said Tab.

"Actually, I already went," I said.

They stopped splashing. A raven squawked overhead.

"Hang on a second," said Tab. "Are you saying you went to this Perpetuum place *just now*?"

I nodded. Tab looked over at Cheese. "And how long were you there?" she asked.

"According to Finn, it doesn't matter," said Cheese. "He's saying he could have been there a month, and it would still only seem like a second to us."

I sat on the bow seat and didn't say anything. I'd definitely been there longer than that.

"Answer the question," said Tab. "How long were you there?"

"I don't know," I said. "Half a year maybe?"

"HALF A YEAR?"

"Something like that. Long enough to — "

Tab put her hands over her ears. She wasn't buying it.

"How's, um, Constant, doing?" Cheese said.

Maybe he wasn't buying it either.

"She's okay," I said. "She's doing all this research on her daughter's illness."

"She has a daughter on the island, too?" said Tab.

"No," I said. "Her daughter's in a hospital."

"So then Constant's on that . . . that *island* all alone?"

"It's not an island," I said. "I told you, it's just the way into Perpetuum."

There was a moment of silence. Water lapped against the side of the boat. Cheese and Tab glanced at each other.

"It sure looks like an island from here," said Tab. "And it looked like an island when I was standing on it, too."

"It looks different from the inside," I repeated. *How many times do I have to tell them that?*

"Yeah, you said that a minute ago. Right before I went ashore and saw absolutely nothing."

That shut me up. There was no way of winning. If the island wasn't a doorway for Tab the way it was for me, there was nothing I could do.

Unless — wait.

Hang on a second.

I shifted to the middle seat. Now I was sitting beside Tab. "Can I borrow your phone?" I asked.

"You can have yours back," Cheese said, handing it over.

"Thanks," I said. "But I need Tab's."

"Uh, okay." She pulled it out of her pocket.

"Excellent," I said. "Now, can I borrow that towel?"

She pulled the towel from around her shoulders. I spread it out on the seat between us. Next, I placed her phone in the centre of the towel and folded it up in a bundle. "Abracadabra," I said, pressing the bundle to my forehead. And then I flung the whole thing into the lake.

"HEY!" cried Tab. "What the heck?"

The towel splashed down, a dozen metres away.

"I'm doing you a favour," I said. "I'm freeing you from the tyranny of time."

Tab punched me in the shoulder — hard. "You idiot," she said. "All my contacts were on that phone."

"Relax," said Cheese. "He palmed it somehow. Your phone's still here in the boat somewhere, right, Finn?"

I was trying not to laugh. It actually worked! They hadn't noticed the misdirect.

"Hey, Tab," I said. "What's that behind your foot?"

She reached down and found her phone.

"Whoa, Finn!" Cheese cried. "Employable skill!"

Tab slipped her phone into her pocket and crossed her arms. "Thank you," she said. "Now where's my towel?"

"Uhhh," I said. "Right over there somewhere." I pointed.

"No it's not," said Cheese, scanning the water. "It sank."

Tab swatted my thigh. Not a friendly swat.

Cheese was laughing. "That was impressive, Finn. Where'd you learn to do that?"

"Constant taught me," I said.

Tab said something under her breath.

"I heard that," I said.

"Good," said Tab.

"I'm really sorry," I said. "I'll buy you a new towel, *I promise.*"

"You'd better," she said. "Plus don't forget my brother's bike."

* * *

That night, after dinner, I collapsed into bed. It felt like months had passed since I'd seen a pillow. They sort of had.

I slept for a few hours, but then a thunderstorm woke me up. It was still far away; more of a vibration than a sound. I lay in the darkness, listening to it rumble toward us. It seemed to come closer, only to fade farther away.

After an hour, the storm still hadn't hit, but the lightning was getting brighter. I still couldn't sleep, so I got dressed and went down to the lake.

Careful, Finn. Don't fall.

I clung to the railing as I felt my way down the steps. The wind was crazy. It sounded like huge sheets of tinfoil were being dragged between the trees.

Finally I reached the lake. Lightning flashed, outlining the far shore. I tried walking on the dock, but it was heaving up and down with the waves, and spray was flying everywhere, so I backed off. I headed back up the ramp and sat with my back propped against the dock box. That was better — more sheltered from the wind.

More lightning. My heart hopscotched. Then came the thunder.

I wished Constant could be here to see this. She often complained about the weather in Perpetuum. The lack of weather, I mean. It never changed. It never rained, never got windy and the sky was always that greyish skim-milk colour.

I worried about the floating island. What would happen if the storm ripped it apart? Would my Glimmer Line get ripped apart, too? If that happened, would I ever get back to Perpetuum?

Almost immediately, the wind dropped away. Which meant the rain was about to hit. I started up the stairs and heard a hissing noise behind me. It was the first fat raindrops, lashing down on the lake. I made it upstairs just as the downpour started. Everybody was asleep. I snuck into my bedroom, my heart pounding.

I was exhilarated now, and more awake than ever, so I sat on the floor with all the lights turned off. My brain was seaplaning, worrying about the island and Cheese and Tab, and whether they would ever believe me about Perpetuum and Constant.

Some time after midnight, Mom got up to go to the bathroom. When she flushed the toilet, the whole cabin shook. I still wasn't tired, so I turned on my light and wrote out a bunch of new lists. Most importantly:

Ten Worst Things About Being Vision Impaired:
–walking through parking lots with fast-moving cars
–bus drivers who forget to call out the stops
–headphone jacks that are too tiny to see
–ditto for USB ports
–ditto for electrical sockets
–text enlargement apps that don't work on Android
–voice recognition software that can't figure out what I'm
    saying
–teachers who think I'm not just low-vision, but also stupid
–not knowing if girls are looking at me
–not seeing Tab's face very clearly

CHAPTER
20

The Back Seat

Seconds until school: 1,472,400
Until Lights Out: 140,378,400

Eventually I fell asleep on the floor, and the next thing I knew, sunshine was streaming through my window. I got to my feet, avoiding the new strings I'd tacked up from one side of the room to the other.

First two thoughts of the day:

Number 1: Brother, it's *hot*.

Number 2: What happened to the island? And what about Perpetuum?

I hunted around in the kitchen for a box of cereal and then I carried it down to the lake. I counted the steps — 270 . . . 271 . . . 272 — and then sat down at the end of the dock.

The sun sprayed oily light over the lake, and the trees were still dripping from the overnight storm. The pump clicked on behind me. Someone else was up.

A family of ducks swam past the dock. I couldn't see them very clearly, but I sure could hear the quacking. I tossed them a handful of cereal and they went totally bonkers. I walked up to the pumphouse to get my fishing rod and a container of worms. Dad had a half-dozen rods in there, and it took forever to find mine among them, but I somehow did.

I went back down to the end of the dock. The ducks had paddled off, so I skewered a worm with my hook and dropped the line into the lake. The fish were biting but they kept stealing my worms. I counted how many I had left. Only three. I sliced them into halves to make them last.

Cheese came down the steps. "Any sign of Tab?" he asked. He was eating something — a slice of watermelon, I think.

"With these eyes?" I said.

"Sorry." He scanned the lake for a few seconds and then sat down beside me.

"If she was thirty metres away, then maybe I'd see her," I said dipping my finger into the lake and tracing a figure eight on the dock. It dried instantly in the sun.

Cheese spat something into the lake. Watermelon seeds, probably. "Freaky day yesterday, eh?" he said.

"Yeah," I muttered. Understatement of the century.

He wiped some juice off his chin. "Can you teach me how to do that magic trick?" he asked.

"Maybe later," I said.

Cheese nodded and took another bite of watermelon. I felt another tug on my line.

"Do you think Tab believes me at all?" I asked.

"I think she does . . . Maybe . . . A bit." Cheese reached forward and did something to his flip-flops. "That Spanish trick was pretty impressive. The magic, too."

I reeled in my line. The fish slipped off the hook. "The Spanish wasn't a trick," I said. "It was hard work."

Cheese tossed the watermelon rind into the lake and

rinsed his hands in the water. "Were you really in Perpetuum for months?" he asked.

"Hard to say," I told him. "It never gets dark there, so you can't really keep track of days. It sure seemed like a long time. How long does it usually take to learn a new language?"

Cheese shrugged and stared at the lake. A fish came up to the surface to grab a water bug and left a dimple in the water. "Depends how committed you are," Cheese said.

"I was pretty committed," I said.

"I bet you were," he said. He poked me in the ribs and we both laughed. He reached for the cereal box and poured himself a handful.

"I didn't stay as long the second time," I said. "But it was long enough to learn a few magic tricks. Plus I built a jump line and a pump track."

"What, for bikes?" said Cheese.

"Yeah," I said.

He didn't laugh, which I hoped was progress. I sliced the remaining half-worms into quarters and rebaited the hook.

"You better pray you don't come back as a worm in your next life," Cheese said, looking at the jackknife in my hand.

"Can't be worse than being blind," I said.

"Worms *are* blind," he said. "Plus, they're worms. So it would definitely be worse."

He took a bottle out of his knapsack and squirted a blob of something onto his hand.

"Is that sunscreen?" I asked.

"Yeah."

"What SPF?"

"Thirty."

I lay down my rod and reached for the bottle.

"Hey," said Cheese. "There she is."

"Tab?"

"Yeah. Paddling her kayak. Over by Seagull Island."

I glanced up, even though I knew I wouldn't see anything. I don't know why I bother. Habit, I guess.

"She's towing a second kayak," said Cheese. "Man, you should see her go."

My line jiggled and I set the bottle down. I gave the rod a jerk. This time the fish stayed on.

"The wind's blowing this way," Cheese said, still looking across the lake. "That's why she's moving so fast."

I reeled in the line and hoisted it into the air. I'd caught a sunfish — 12 centimetres or so.

"Thorny And Beautiful," I said.

"The fish?"

"No, our friend Tab. T-A-B. Stands for *thorny and beautiful.*"

I held the sunfish in one hand, brushed back its spines and wiggled the hook out of its mouth.

"You like her, don't you?" Cheese asked.

I released the fish back into the lake. "T-A-B," I replied. "Type A Behaviour."

"T-A-B," said Cheese. "Totally Awesome Babe."

I rinsed the slime off my hands. It didn't matter if I liked her or not. No way would she go for a guy with my problems. No way.

"I don't care one way or the other," said Cheese. "It's just that . . . Oh, never mind."

Is he jealous? What is going on?

159

"What?" I said. *Spit it out, buddy.*

"It's just . . . You can be a bit intense. You should try acting more relaxed, if you can."

Easy for you to say, I thought. Problems seemed to pass through Cheese like the breeze.

I stared at the shoreline. It was a blurry wall of green, except for one tree that hung over the lake at a weird angle.

"Like, your obsession with the floating island," Cheese said. "I've seen it three times, so maybe it's easier for me to try to believe. It's harder for Tab. I mean, *time standing still?* Hello? That's a lot for anyone to absorb."

I thought: *I'm always going to be like that tree. Standing alone, at a freaky angle.* I knew this like bike tires knew mud. Some trees are doomed to stand alone.

"You believe me, don't you?" I asked.

Cheese finished rubbing the sunscreen onto his arms. "I believe something weird is going on," he said. "I'm just not sure what it means."

He reached for the cereal box again. "I know you didn't speak Spanish before this week. And I never saw you do magic before, either. But does that mean there's a magical island where time stands still?"

He poured himself a handful of cereal. "We're friends, Finn, but Tab doesn't know you as well as I do. So you might want to tone down the floating island stuff a bit."

I sighed and reached for my container of worms. "It's not your problem," I said.

"I know it isn't," said Cheese. "And yet, for some reason, I still want to help. Hmmm, I wonder why that is."

"Because you're a masochist?" I said.

"No," said Cheese. "The correct term is rock star."

He elbowed me in the ribs. I elbowed him back. Then we started wrestling, until the worms landed in the cereal box.

* * *

Tab arrived, towing the extra kayak. It had two seats, which meant we could all go paddling together.

Tab gave the single-seater to Cheese, so I climbed into the back of the double. At first I felt a bit like a seabird — with half my body underwater and half above. The kayak wobbled at the slightest movement. I was afraid to sneeze, for fear of flipping the thing.

Tab was standing at the end of the dock. "Hold the paddle with both hands," she told Cheese. "That's it, arms out, collarbone height. Perfect. Now roll your shoulders. Yeah, keep doing that."

That's right. Cheese, who's terrified of water, somehow got a kayak all to himself. Not me, even though I've got a lifesaving badge. I had to be chauffeured by a girl.

Get used to it, buddy. This is your life. You're always going to be the guy in the back seat.

Tab nudged Cheese's kayak away from the dock with her foot.

"What if I want to turn?" he yelped.

"Paddle extra hard on one side."

The kayak scissored through the water. Tab started clapping. "Nice," she said. "Now, equal pressure on both sides."

T-A-B, I thought: *Thoroughly Able Boater.*

She walked over to me and said, "Ready to go?"

"Let's do it," I said.

The *swish-swish* of Cheese's paddle faded away. Tab slid

into the cockpit ahead of mine and used her paddle to shove us away from the dock.

I took a couple of awkward strokes. Cheese suddenly appeared right beside us.

"Easy!" I said. I'd nearly clocked him in the head.

"Sorry," he squeaked. "This vessel has a mind of its own."

"Aim for the third bridge," Tab instructed.

"Yes, ma'am!" Cheese slashed at the water.

Little waves drummed against the side of our kayak. "This feels supremely weird," I said to Tab.

"Don't worry," she said. "You'll get the hang of it in no time."

The kayak felt even tippier than the canoe. It felt like we could capsize at any moment.

"I can feel the wave action on my butt," I said.

"Overshare," said Tab. "Keep your elbows tight."

We stayed close to shore until we passed Seagull Island, and then we moved out into the open lake. A motorboat was buzzing around in Bully Bay. The engine kept making high-pitched squawks, which meant it was going around in tight circles.

"Wow, they're good," Tab said.

"Who's good?"

"Those water skiers. Can you see them?"

"No."

"Oh. Well, they're awesome. They're sending up huge rooster tails of spray."

I could picture it.

"When did you find out about your eyes?" Tab said, her voice dropping an octave lower than normal.

"Officially, last January," I said.

"*Officially?*"

"I sort of knew a long time before that."

"How's that?" Tab asked.

I took another stroke and rested my paddle. "Two years ago I blew through a stop sign on my bike. A cop was there and pulled me over."

"A cop stopped you *on your bike?*" Tab asked.

"I live in Edmonton," I said. "They hate cyclists there. Anyway, the cop asked if I'd seen the stop sign, which I hadn't."

Tab nodded. "So . . . did you go to an eye doctor after that?"

"Of course not," I said. "That would've been smart. And as everyone knows, I'm not very smart. No, I just kept riding my bike. And then, a couple months later, I ran into an old man."

"WHAT?" said Tab. "You *hit* an old man with your bike?"

"Yeah," I said, embarrassed.

"Was he hurt?"

It was a crappy thing to have to remember. "They thought he'd broken his hip at first," I said. "But he turned out to be fine."

"How old was he?"

"I don't know. Eighty?" I started paddling again.

"So you went to the eye doctor after that, right?" Tab asked.

I shook my head. "No, I didn't. When stuff like that happens, you don't automatically think, *I'm going blind.* I figured I was just having a run of bad luck."

I pulled my goodie bag out of the cockpit and ate a handful of trail mix. I passed the bag forward to Tab.

"Where's Cheese got to?" I asked.

"Way ahead. He's almost at the bridge."

Tab took a handful of nuts and passed the bag back. I stuffed it down beside my legs.

"So what happened after that?" Tab asked. "How did you find out the truth about your eyes?"

Deep breath. "Um . . . I rode my bike off a cliff."

"You — what?" She turned around.

"Yeah. Pretty stupid, I know. I thought it was just a bend in the trail. But no. It turned out to be a cliff."

A spear of colour appeared down the lake. A sailboat? Had to be.

"Are you talking about Drag River?" Tab asked.

"You know about that?"

"Cheese mentioned it, yeah."

I ran my tongue over my teeth. There was a coppery taste in my mouth, as if I'd been sucking on loose change.

"What exactly did Cheese tell you?" I asked.

"Just that you had an accident. And that's how the two of you became friends."

Funny, I thought. *That Cheese is a riot.*

"Were you hurt?" Tab asked.

"Depends on your definition of hurt," I said. "If a few broken ribs and hypothermia count as hurt, then yeah."

"Oh, please," she said. "That's such a guy thing to say."

"Sorry," I said. "I just — I haven't talked about it very much."

Tab turned around and we went back to paddling. My right hand started twitching for some reason.

"Did Cheese mention that he saved my life?" I asked.

Tab stopped paddling. "No," she said, after a moment. "He did not."

Figures, I thought. *Cheese never talks about that day. He actually apologized to me when the newspaper story came out. He thought I'd be mad because he answered some reporter's questions.*

If our roles had been reversed, and I'd pulled *him* from a frozen river, I would've bragged about it non-stop.

"He didn't even know it was me," I told Tab. "It was December, and I was wearing all sorts of gear. Coat, helmet, goggles, knee pads, shin protectors. That stuff weighs a lot, too. Especially when it's soaking wet."

Tab turned around and looked at me. Strands of her hair lifted up in the breeze.

"The police said the current would've pulled me under the ice," I said. "I probably would have drowned if Cheese hadn't pulled me out."

Tab stared at me, and her face looked different from yesterday. She believed me this time. That was the difference.

"Did you go to the hospital?" she asked.

"Just for one night," I said. "The next day, when I was discharged, my dad drove me back to the trail where it happened. He wanted to know how I could've ridden off the cliff. There were plenty of warning signs around. You seriously had to be blind to miss them.

"Dad kept saying, 'What were you doing here *really*? Were you drinking? Doing drugs? Tell the *truth!*'

"Later on, he felt pretty bad about that. But at the time, I guess it seemed more plausible to him than the alternative."

The water beneath the kayak changed from dark blue to yellow. It was the sun, reflecting off the sandy lake bottom. We were getting close to shore.

"So you rode your bike off a cliff and broke some ribs," Tab said. "Please tell me that you got your eyes checked after that?"

"Yeah, that pretty much did the trick." I laughed. "The day I got diagnosed was pretty crappy, but at least it answered a lot of questions. I was going blind, sure, but at least I wasn't a liar. I wasn't any of those things my dad accused me of."

Tab said nothing. I wished I hadn't opened my mouth. It felt like I'd poked a hole in the kayak, and now a flood of bad feelings was spilling in.

"Sorry," I said. "I'm not usually such a downer."

"It's okay," said Tab. "It's better than bottling it up. Watch your head. Here comes the bridge."

A moment later we floated under the wooden span. Birds swooped back and forth through the archway, centimetres above our heads.

"See the nests?" said Tab.

"No, not really."

"There are dozens of them," said Tab. "Barn swallows. Must have eggs in the nests. That's why they're freaking out."

The birds were winging in and out, shrieking wildly.

"Don't worry," Tab told the birds. "We're leaving, we're leaving."

We coasted out the other side of the bridge. The river opened up before us.

"Where's Cheese?" I asked.

"Over there by the bend."

I couldn't see him clearly, but someone was barbecuing meat. My stomach rumbled. The sun went behind a cloud.

Cheese's voice echoed off the riverbank. "Hey, guys! Check this out."

I heard the *swish-swish* of his paddle. A minute later he swept in beside us. Something red was strewn over the bow of his kayak.

"Check out these maple branches," he said. "The leaves are changing colour already!"

CHAPTER 21

The Universal Categorization System

Seconds until school: 1,429,200
Until Lights Out: 140,335,200

We spent the rest of the day together, kayaking and swimming, and exploring Blueberry Island. The subject of Perpetuum didn't come up once. That was a relief. No awkward conversations.

Toward the end of the afternoon, I invited Tab back to Splitsville. Mistake number 1.

But it wasn't as disastrous as Mistake number 2. I never should've let her see my room.

"Wow, uh, this is, *interesting*," said Tab, ducking under the strings and squeezing in beside the dresser. "What do you call it again?"

"The Universal Categorization System," I said.

"UCS for short," Cheese added. "Which, coincidentally, also stands for Ultra-Crazy Sociopath."

Tab ignored this. Which was pretty generous, considering my bedroom looked like a serial killer's hangout.

"You're making a list of *everything* in the universe?" she asked.

"That's the plan," I said. "Of course, I'm just getting started. And it's not scientific or anything. Another person would build it differently."

I'd broken the universe down into two main categories: *Physical* things and *Non-physical* things.

Physical things went on the north-facing wall. *Non-physical* stuff went on the south. At the top of the *Physical* wall, I had three big headings: *Animal, Vegetable* and *Mineral*.

"Watch that string," said Cheese. "There, by your fore-head."

"Thanks," said Tab, ducking down.

I'd broken the *Non-physical* wall into four categories: *Religion, Philosophy, Emotions* and *Dreams*.

Some things didn't fit into any of those groups, but seemed to belong somewhere in between. Exercise, for instance. It's not *Animal, Vegetable* or *Mineral*, but I thought it should be connected to the *Physical* wall somehow. So I ran a string from one side of the room to the other, from *The Human Body* on the north wall to *Meditation* on the south. I stuck the *Exercise* sticky note right in the middle.

After that, things had spun out of control. I tacked a bunch of other strings from one side of the room to the other and then added a bunch more notes. My two-dimensional list became a 3-D word cloud. My room looked like a giant spiderweb, the airspace clotted with hundreds of notes.

"Hey," Tab said. "This is interesting."

"What?" I asked.

"A whole section on girls."

"Right," said Cheese. "That's my cue to leave." He walked across the hall to his room.

"Where are you going?" Tab asked him.

He reappeared with a pink Hula Hoop. He was also wearing headphones. "I've got a date with Mozart," he said, grinning.

He walked away. "What does that mean?" Tab asked.

"He has to Hula Hoop to one of Mozart's symphonies. It's forty minutes long. It's for some online contest."

The screen door swung open and then closed.

"He's going to Hula Hoop for forty minutes?" said Tab.

"He's been practising all week," I explained. "He's actually pretty good."

"I'll bet," said Tab. "You, on the other hand, need help. Why'd you put *Girls* in this remote galaxy?"

"What galaxy is that?" I asked.

"*Things I Do Not Know*."

Great, just great.

"It's not that I don't know girls," I said. "It's just that I sometimes get shy when they're around."

It wasn't always that way. I used to be Mr. Popular. But that all got torpedoed by my eyeballs.

"Could've fooled me," she said. She stepped around the dresser and read some of the notes beside the window. I could hear Cheese panting outside.

"Who's Spencer?" Tab asked.

"Huh?"

"This note says, *Spencer / Skid Marks*. It's lumped under the category, *Relationship Fails*."

Oh, right. That.

"Spencer used to be my best friend," I said.

"He ditched you?" Tab asked.

I didn't answer. Couldn't.

I still remembered the text I'd sent him.

Sorry, no time.

Back in the day, when we were still friends, I used to ask Spencer for help — like, twenty times a day. Help reading my assignments, help with ZoomText, help tightening the spokes on my bike. But here's the thing: I could never return the favour. I could never help *him* with anything. Because of my eyes.

I got to feeling pretty guilty about it. So I did him a favour. I backed out of his life.

The next time he asked me to hang out at the mall, I sent him that text: *Sorry, no time.*

I sent him that same text over and over, whenever he suggested we hang out.

Sorry, no time. Sorry, no time.

Eventually Spencer got the message. That was the real reason he wasn't my friend anymore.

He hadn't ditched me. I'd ditched *him* first, so he wouldn't have to.

Tab sat down on a corner of the bed. I hadn't answered her question, but she didn't seem to notice. "You know this is a bit intense, right?" she said, looking around.

"I know," I said. "But I need to keep busy. It takes my mind off other stuff."

I could still hear Cheese Hula Hooping outside. Tab leaned over and peeked out the window. She tapped on the glass and waved. Then she swivelled back toward me.

"What was Cheese doing down at the river that day?" she asked. "You know, when he pulled you out of the ice?"

"He was hiking with his dad," I said. "They live in an apartment, not far from the water treatment plant."

Tab picked up my guitar and pushed it down the bed toward me. "Play something," she said.

"No way," I said.

"Why not?"

"Because I'm no good."

"I don't believe you. Cheese says you're good."

I took the guitar. "I'm just a noodler," I said.

"So noodle," she said. "I'll just listen."

I sat down on the edge of the bed and strummed a bit, and the two of us kept talking as I played.

"Did you know Cheese very well before that?" she asked.

"Not really," I said. "We sort of travelled in different circles."

The longer we talked, the more relaxed I felt. The more relaxed I got, the better I played.

"You're definitely not a noodler," said Tab. "You play like a pro. Hey, I know that tune. It's Wolf Willow, right? I knew it. 'As the Crow Flies.'"

The girl knew her music!

"That is a total jam," she said, scrunching her back against the wall. "Hey, what's your favourite song?"

"I don't really have a favourite," I said. "But this one is right up there . . . "

I played it as well as I could. Tab didn't recognize it.

"It's old," I said. "The original has lots of horns."

I played the chorus again. She still didn't recognize it.

"What is it?" said Tab.

"'Sir Duke' by Stevie Wonder," I said. "It's, like, a *detonation* of joy. My dad and I used to dance to it when I was little."

Yes, believe it or not, my dad used to dance. He did lame dad-dancing. But still. He liked to dance.

Tab's foot was bobbing to the music. I played the chorus a third time.

Tab hugged a pillow to her chest. "Isn't Stevie Wonder blind?" she asked.

"Yeah," I said. "He was born premature and his retinas detached. He never had any sight at all."

"Do you know any more of his songs?"

I thought for a second, and then played "You Are the Sunshine of My Life."

"I know that one," Tab said. "It's kind of meh."

I wished that I could see her face better. Her voice sounded like she was smiling, but I couldn't be sure. Cheese was still going strong with the Hula Hoop. I lost the thread of the Stevie song and went back to noodling. This guitar wasn't anywhere as good as the one Constant had given me. Still, the steel strings sounded great, and I'd developed calluses on my fingers.

I played another song: "Between the Bones" by MPSQ. Suddenly Tab said, "You told me yesterday you couldn't play that song."

Had I? I strained to remember. Yesterday had been a very long day.

"I didn't know how to play the song *then*," I explained. "But that was before I went back to Perpetuum."

Tab looked at me, but didn't say anything.

"Constant gave me some guitar lessons while I was there," I said.

More silence. "But you just played the guitar solo better than on the record."

"I practised a lot," I said.

Cheese was still huffing and puffing on the deck. Splitsville was shaking on its stilts a little bit.

"Time stretches there," I reminded Tab. "One second here is maybe like a year there."

Tab stood up and looked out the window. A few seconds went by and neither of us spoke. She started to say something, stopped, took a deep breath. Finally she said, "You don't have to do this, you know."

"Do what?"

"I don't blame you for wanting to run away. I'd want the same thing if I was losing most of my eyesight."

"Yeah, well."

She turned around. "You've had a big shock, Finn. And it's important to talk this stuff out. But from what I can see, this floating island thing isn't helping. One of my brothers suffers from depression and — "

Oh — I got it now. She didn't believe me *at all*. She still thought I was making everything up. Perpetuum, Constant. The magic lessons. Even the guitar playing.

"I mean, my brother — " Tab went on.

"I don't want to talk about this," I snapped.

"You can call it Perpetuum or whatever you want. But I'll tell you what it really is. It's avoidance."

T-A-B: *Throws A Bomb!*

I could feel my eyelid twitching.

174

"Cause I'm that kind of guy, right?" I said. "The kind of guy who lies to his friends?"

Tab said nothing. I felt sick to my stomach.

"Yeah, you've totally got me pegged," I said, setting the guitar on the floor. "I'm a compulsive liar. Worse. A useless, lying freak show."

Have I mentioned how awful it is to be going blind? How you're always making dumb mistakes because you can't read people's faces clearly? If I'd seen what Tab's face looked like right then, I might have said something different, and saved everyone a lot of trouble. But I said what I said, and a moment later, Tab stomped out, snapping a bunch of UCS strings in her path. She tossed the pillow she'd been holding onto the bed, leaving a little crater in the bedspread.

CHAPTER
22

Pain Bomb

Seconds until school: 1,427,400
Until Lights Out: 140,333,400

Everything went downhill fast after that.

The evening.

The holiday.

My whole stupid life.

First I texted Minnow. Because I'm idiotic that way. I had this sudden urge to be rejected *yet again*.

Hey you, I typed. *Whats goin on?* SEND.

She was there. I could see her active account.

Howz ur smmr so far? SEND.

Wait. Wait. Still no reply.

My dendrites call out for your company. SEND. That was Cheese's line, but there's no way she'd know that.

Still no reply. What was she doing?

Then I realized: She was wishing I'd stop bugging her. Wishing I'd stop acting like a psycho stalker.

Back in the fall, before we started hanging out, I texted her a poem I wrote. She liked it, I guess, because she texted back: *Poems R 4 frnds & bfrnds & cardboard boxes.*

I spent 60 seconds trying to decipher what that meant. Until she sent this nerve-jangling postscript:

Which R U? Frnd or bfrnd or cardboard box?

BAM. Game over. We were a couple the next day. She told all her friends I was her "cardboard box."

Now, all these months later, I looked over what I'd written:

Don't u miss ur crdbrd bx?

I know, pathetic. But oh well. SEND.

Nothing. Nothing. Nothing. Wait. The blinking blue light. Her cheerful response: *FINN STOP IT JST GO AWAY.*

I sat on the bed, barely breathing. After a minute, I grabbed my Sharpie. I wrote the word *Minnow* on a note. Then I pressed it to the wall, alongside the other *Things I Do Not Know.*

Another message pinged my inbox. A teeny bit warmer this time.

SORRY. BUT PLZ STOP. TIME HEALS. M.

Deep breath. In and out.

Without warning, Cheese pushed open my bedroom door. "Things okay between you and Tab?" he asked.

"No comment," I said.

"She left kind of fast."

"No comment."

"And you're sitting here by yourself."

I glared at him.

"What?" he said.

"Nothing," I said. "I mean, you're right. Tab isn't my biggest fan at the moment."

He leaned back against the door, still holding his Hula Hoop. A stripe of sunlight crossed his face and his hair lit up like a forest fire.

"Minnow hates me, too," I said. "You have to help me, Cheese. What am I doing wrong?"

He *boinged* the doorstopper with his foot. "You should stop seeing girls named after fish."

What's that supposed to mean?

"That makes absolutely no sense," I said.

"Sure it does," said Cheese. "Tab's last name is Coley. Which is a type of pollock. Or maybe a flounder. Some fish, anyway."

"You're joking," I said.

"Sadly, I'm not." He sat on the floor and peeled off his purple headband. "Don't forget, you've got a fishy name, too," he went on. "Maybe you subconsciously want to be with your own kind."

I had a fishy name? Oh yeah, Finn.

"Did you finish your video?" I asked.

"No, my phone died. Is yours charged? I have to do it over."

"You have to do the *whole thing* again?"

"Yeah. But it's only forty minutes."

Like I said. Worst day ever. Cheese Hula Hooping to Mozart for 40 minutes. That's right up there.

Out in the living room, the land line rang. Mom picked up and started gabbing, so Cheese and I went down to the lake. He ran, and I followed slowly, holding the railing.

"Let's shoot the video right here," Cheese said at the top of the ramp. "That way we'll have the dock, and the sunset in the background."

I propped my phone on a wicker chair and made sure Cheese was in the frame.

"Musiknerd.com doesn't really care if I go for the full forty minutes," Cheese said. "They just want a video of a skinny brown kid Hula Hooping to Mozart's 'Jupiter' symphony."

"You okay with that?" I asked.

Cheese shrugged. "International fame is international fame. Besides, I don't use my real name. I go by Cheddar Man online."

He snapped his headphones over his ears. I hit the record button. "Three . . . two . . . one . . . Action!"

Cheese started the music on his player and three loud bursts of orchestral music bled through his headphones. He started wiggling his hips.

I double-checked to make sure the red light on my phone was flashing, and then I grabbed my fishing rod and went down to the dock. Tab had left her two-seater kayak behind.

The sun broke through the clouds and painted a yellow stripe on the far shore. It looked a bit cartoony. Sunsets always made the world look like an animated movie. I half-expected Buzz Lightyear to go flying past.

I tied a lure to my line and cast it into the lake. After a while, I heard voices coming down the steps.

"Catch anything?" Dad called.

"No," I said.

He was coming down the stairs with Mom. They said hi to Cheese, but he was deep in the zone and didn't reply. Dad was wearing his usual summer gear: puffy vest, plaid shorts and Velcro sandals with white socks.

"Who was that on the phone?" I asked.

"You'll never guess," said Dad.

The clouds clamped shut like a garage door coming down. The trees on the far shore faded to grey.

"It's good news," said Mom.

"My school burned down?" I asked.

Dad snorted.

They were standing right behind me now.

"I landed that job at the hospital," Mom said.

"Cool," I said, looking back at Cheese. He'd been going for 10 minutes.

"There's just one hitch," Dad said, slinging an arm around Mom's shoulder. *Wow*, I thought, *we're touchy-touchy tonight.*

"They want me to start right away," Mom said. "First thing Wednesday morning."

"Cool," I said. I'd miss her, but I'd survive.

Mom and Dad glanced at each other.

"We've decided to go back Tuesday night," Dad said. "It'll be easier all around since we've only got the one car."

"Tuesday? But we're staying here until Labour Day," I said. "That's still two weeks away."

"Change of plans," said Dad, looking up the ramp. "Cheese should let his folks know that he'll be coming home early."

Today was already Sunday. That meant we had less than two days — which was . . . 172 thousand seconds.

No. Not possible. Twelve days of holiday — *gone?*

And why? Because of a stupid job?

"Can't you take a bus?" I asked Mom.

"We checked," she said. "There's only one — and it's tonight. I'd have to be in Dyer's Bay by ten."

What time is it now? Must be around eight. "We could still make it," I said.

"No we couldn't," said Mom. "I haven't packed."

"I can help with that," I said. "Let's do it now!"

Oh, God. Move! Move!

"Calm down, Finn," Dad said.

"I'll have you packed in no time," I said. "Hey, Cheese, time to take a break!"

I ran up the ramp and grabbed his Hula Hoop.

"Hey!" he shouted. "I'm only on the second movement."

"I need your help," I said.

"Finn, slow down." That was Dad.

"I can take care of this," I said. "I just need to — "

I'd turned and started up the stairs, but my foot went down weird and then I was sprawling sideways. Something smashed hard against my knee.

"Finn!"

Grenades went off. Grenades of pain.

My vision narrowed to a tiny blue tunnel. My peripheral vision faded to black and blanked out.

171,800 seconds until we left for home.

171,799.

171,798.

Slowly, colour drifted back into the world. "That's it," I heard my dad say. "Breathe deep. Good man."

I was lying sideways on the ground, clutching my leg. I think I was crying. Oh yeah — I was definitely crying.

"Let me see that knee," Mom said.

I took my hands off the knee, then quickly put them back. "I think that step is loose," I said.

Mom reached under my shoulder and helped me sit up. Her grip felt good, like a tight coil of rope.

"Seriously," I said. "That step is loose."

Dad nodded. "I think you're in shock, buddy."

Well, that explains the shivering, I thought. It was a hot summer night, but my body felt like ice.

"We have to get Mom packed," I told Cheese. "Otherwise we'll have to go home in two days."

"We can talk about that later," Mom said. "Right now we need to get you upstairs."

My palms were burning. There was an ice pick in my knee.

"Do you think he'll need any stitches?" Cheese asked.

"I doubt it," said Mom. "But let's help him upstairs and get him cleaned up."

They pulled me to my feet and gripped me under my shoulders. When the three of us got up to the deck, I sat down on the plastic recliner. Mom spread a wine-coloured towel under my leg. I didn't know why at first. Then I saw the drip-drip-drip.

Dad shouted up the hill from below, "These steps aren't loose. He just couldn't see them."

CHAPTER
23

Blind Alley

Seconds until departure: 118,800

It was a thousand-to-one chance. A million-to-one. That's my excuse. I never really thought it would work.

It was the morning after Mom dropped the news about her job. I woke up with a headache, a stomach ache, a brain ache.

Everything ached. Everything felt black.

What was wrong with me?

Flu?

Food poisoning?

Then I remembered.

Tab hates me.

The holiday's over.

We're going home tomorrow. In less than 33 hours.

Put more exactly: 118,800 seconds.

118,799.

118,798.

I rolled out of bed. YOW! Who hammered that steak knife into my knee?

And why was everything so dark?

I pushed myself to my feet and stood up. I could smell

coffee brewing, but the sun wasn't up. My eyelids felt like they were made of birch bark, and they scratched my eyes every time I tried to blink. I hobbled toward the window and snapped one of my *UCS* lines.

Could things get worse? I wondered.

Yes, they definitely could.

I reached the window and went to open the curtains. But surprise, surprise! They were already open.

Great, just great. It was 7:30 in the morning. Either we'd had a nuclear disaster, or my vision had cratered during the night.

My veins filled with ice. I wanted to scream. This wasn't supposed to happen for five more years.

I opened my door. Heard voices in the kitchen.

"How'd you sleep, Tiger?" said Mom.

She was somewhere to my left. "Brilliant," I lied. "Hey, what happened to the light?"

"What do you mean?" She sounded alarmed. I could just make her out by the shape of her hair.

"Is there a solar eclipse or something?" I asked.

"Not that I know of. How come?"

"It's just . . . Nothing."

I felt my way past the couch. My peripheral vision was still online, but barely.

118,629 seconds until departure.

118,628.

"How's the knee this morning?" Mom asked.

"Okay," I lied, standing against the window. Second lie in less than two minutes.

I felt woozy, like I hadn't eaten in a week. I slunk back into my room and lay down on my bed. That was better. Wait a second, no it wasn't. The bed was spinning like a merry-go-round.

Suddenly I needed to throw up. And bawl my eyes out. And scream at the moon.

What was happening? What was happening to my eyes? Oh, yes — excellent. Now I was hyperventilating too.

Calm down, I told myself. *Listen to your music. Chill.*

I felt around for my phone. Couldn't find it.

Deep breathing then.

Yeah, like that's going to happen.

For a second I wished Mom would come into the room and curl me up in a blanket and tell me that I'd be fine. "Think of it as turbulence on a plane," she'd told me once. "It feels awful and you're convinced the plane is about to crash, but it isn't. The plane is fine. It's just unsettled air."

118,203.

118,202.

Someone was standing outside my door. The footsteps were too light to belong to my mom.

"You okay in there, Finn?" said Cheese.

NO! my brain screamed. *I'm nowhere near okay! I'm going blind! I'm losing my mind!*

I felt so messed up. I was a waste of human skin. I was an RV park after a tornado had roared through.

My bedroom door creaked open. Cheese came in and stood by the side of the bed.

"How bad is it?" he whispered. "On a scale of one to ten?"

"One hundred and eighteen thousand," I muttered.

* * *

The bed-spins eventually passed, and I stopped hyperventilating, but then I fell asleep and had all these crazy nightmares. I was a Rice Krispie being chased by a huge jug of milk. It wanted to splash me and make me go POP. Then I was surfing on a collapsing condo tower. Then I was being eaten by a lobster the size of a rhinoceros.

Crazy stuff. When I blasted awake, I found my phone and checked the time. My vision was still sketchy, but there was more light in my bedroom than before. Things weren't quite so blurry, either, thank goodness. Hopefully the vision loss was just a temporary thing.

I staggered into the kitchen and grabbed a slice of bread and some milk. Then I went outside onto the deck.

Cheese was reading in the hammock. "How're you feeling now?" he asked.

"Pretty spaced out," I said.

He dropped the book to his chest. "Your mom told me to keep an eye on you," he said.

"Where *is* she?"

"Up the hill with your dad. They were acting kind of strange. They had a phone call with Mrs. Coley."

"Tab's mom?"

Cheese nodded.

That can't be good, I thought.

"What did they talk about?"

He shrugged. "No idea. It was actually Tab who called. She wanted to talk to you."

"What for?"

"I think she felt bad about last night," Cheese said. "I told her you were in bed. She said she'd call back."

A yellow, plastic bag was lying on the deck. I reached down to pick it up.

"Then her mom came on the line," Cheese went on. "She wanted to speak to your parents for some reason."

What could that be about? Had Tab told them that I'd lost her brother's bike? She'd said the Snakebite wasn't worth very much. Could she be wrong? Was I on the hook for more than a hundred bucks?

"What are you doing?" Cheese asked suddenly.

I was crouched down, feeling around for the plastic bag, but now I realized there wasn't anything there. It was just a scrap of sunlight, flickering on the deck. I stood up and brushed my hands against my pants.

"I'm going down to the dock," I sighed. "Think I'll stick my head in the water."

"Is your vision any better?" Cheese asked.

"Tiny bit," I said.

"Good," said Cheese.

I started down the steps, clutching the railing. *Tomorrow,* I thought. *We're leaving tomorrow. In less than 33 hours. Not much more than 100,000 seconds.*

When I got to the dock, I splashed water over my head, and then I lay down on my back with my T-shirt draped over my face. The sun was hotter than a blast furnace. A storm was coming. Had to be.

Great, I thought. *Another storm. This one will probably rip the floating island to pieces and wreck my Glimmer Line for good.*

I pulled the T-shirt off my face. Our motorboat bobbed up and down beside the dock. Tab's kayak tugged at its ropes, too. I could see flashes of whitecaps on the bay.

Wouldn't it be wild, I suddenly thought, *if I paddled up the lake to Tab's place on my own . . . If I found the Organ Donor, hiked to Mislaid Lake and then took the rowboat to Perpetuum — by myself.*

There it was. My crazy idea.

Then I thought: *No. Don't even think it. Too dangerous. It's too windy. There's a storm coming. Plus your vision is even crappier than usual.*

Besides, there was zero per cent chance of success. Even if I miraculously made it to Tab's cottage, I'd never make it across her lawn to the Organ Donor without being spotted.

Right. A boneheaded idea. I splashed more water on my face.

And yet, her kayak was *sitting right there*. And this was the last chance I'd ever have to go back.

All I had to do was slip on a life jacket, and . . .

106,273.

106,272.

106,271.

Why not try? I thought. *I've got nothing to lose. If I get caught, I'll just say I went out for a paddle and got lost.*

But what if something bad happened? What if I got lost — or drowned?

106,240.

106,239.

On the other hand, what if I made it? Then I wouldn't ever have to go back to school. I wouldn't have to face Spencer or Minnow. And I'd never have to worry about stumbling around with a white cane.

That's it, I decided. *I'm doing this.* I pulled on a life jacket and untied the ropes.

* * *

My biggest fear was that I'd smash into a rock and have to buy Tab's parents a new kayak. I was already on the hook for the lost bike and Tab's towel, but that was nothing compared to what a kayak would cost.

Add it to my bill, I thought as I paddled into the waves, fighting the wind. The bow of the kayak pitched up and down. I tried to stay close to shore, but I kept losing sight of it.

I paddled for an hour; then 90 minutes. Most of the time, the kayak barely seemed to be moving.

It doesn't matter, I told myself. *You always knew this wouldn't work. You're just out here for a relaxing paddle, remember?*

100,839.

100,838.

My shoulders were burning and my knee was throbbing from the fall the night before. And I was wishing I'd brought along some food. Even one of Mom's gluten-free granola bars would've been okay.

As I paddled, I kept wondering what Mrs. Coley had said to my parents. Was I really in trouble? Or was she calling about something else? Maybe she just wanted one of Mom's vegan recipes. Or maybe she needed the kayak back.

Suddenly, to my left, I heard waves crashing against rocks. *Has to be an island,* I thought. There weren't many islands at this end of the lake. If I was lucky, it was the one across the bay from Tab's place.

I swung the kayak to the right and paddled hard. Not

long after that, I heard someone shouting.

"Hey, you! Bring it in over here! I'll catch you!"

It was some guy on shore, wearing a red shirt. Relieved, I paddled toward him. When I got close enough, he grabbed my bow and tied the line to a dock.

"Thanks," I said, hopping out.

"No problem," the man said. "It's a bit windy for kayaking."

He wasn't wearing a red shirt after all. He was shirtless. His chest was as red as a beet.

"It's a bit crazy out there," I admitted.

I told him I was looking for the Coleys' cabin — and he told me they lived just six lots over. I played the blind card and let it drop about my eyesight. The guy acted like a miracle had happened.

"Really?" he said. "You paddled all that way on your *own*?"

I nodded.

"You can leave your kayak here if you want," he said. "Want me to show you the way?"

"NO!" I said. "I mean, no thanks. I can find it."

Shirtless man clapped me hard on the back, which made me glad I was still wearing my life jacket. "Like to be independent, I see. That's really great. Good for you."

Time check:

100,418 seconds.

100,417.

I thanked him and walked along the shoreline, still wearing my bright red life jacket. Terrible camouflage, but it couldn't be helped. I was going to need it if I ever got to Mislaid Lake.

I found a treeline and followed it up the slope to the woods. Then I hiked farther east, counting cabins as I passed. After the fourth cabin, I saw something moving. Cougar? Grizzly? I backed into the forest. The brown spot disappeared.

I waited for 10 seconds, and then POW! Skyforce's paws were up on my shoulders.

I tried to push him down, but it didn't work. "Down, Skyforce!" I hissed. "I said, *get down!*"

The dog went into a crouch and thumped his tail against the dirt.

I backed away and he exploded again, running around my legs, barking like crazy.

"Skyforce! Hey, Skyforce! Where are you, boy?"

Tab's voice. Skyforce froze and then raced away. Relieved, I slunk backwards into the forest.

"There you are!" I heard Tab say in the distance. "What was that all about? Did you smell a bear?"

Somehow, she hadn't noticed my life jacket. I stood still for a few minutes. Her voice faded away.

I turned around and pushed deeper into the woods — and spotted a brown stripe of dirt.

There it is, I thought. *That's the trail.*

The Organ Donor. Had to be.

I hiked along the trail, going as fast as I could manage, i.e. not very fast at all.

99,730.

99,729.

A sticky breeze raced through the forest. The sky seemed to have gotten lower. It was being pressed down by a column of purple clouds.

I kept walking into the forest. From time to time, ugly thoughts filled my head. Like, *Are you sure you want to do this,*

Finn? People get lost out here and die in these mountains every year. And those are people who have 20/20 vision.

Yeah, yeah, whatever, I thought. *Ain't nothing gonna break my stride.*

One great thing about being a compulsive counter: I knew exactly how far I had to walk. The last time I was here, with Cheese and Tab, I'd counted my steps on the walk home. That's how I knew it was 3,107 steps between Tab's place and the spot where we'd joined the trail above Mislaid Lake.

Sure enough, after 2,963 steps, the trail went down a hill that was covered with roots. It seemed familiar, and I figured it had to be the spot where I'd crashed Tab's brother's bike. It felt like years had passed since then. As hard as it was to believe, it had only been two days.

Wait — what was that sound? An airplane?

No, it was thunder. The sun slipped behind a cloud.

I looked back and forth. Yeah, this was the place. Mislaid Lake was a straight shot down the hill. I started working my way down, feeling the slope of the ground. Whenever the ground tipped down, I knew I was going the right way. When it tilted up, I turned around and doubled back until I started going down again.

Man, it was hot. The air was as damp as a sweaty gym sock.

Another crunch of thunder — closer this time. Then a skull-cracking flash of light.

Whoa — that hurt! I clamped my eyes shut. When I opened them again, I staggered forward and down, forward and down. I knew Mislaid Lake was close — I could hear waves smashing against the shore. The trees bent almost double in the wind and then sprang back.

Suddenly my shoulder snapped sideways. But it was just a tree, trying to occupy the same space, at the same time, as my body.

I brushed myself off and stood back up. *Should've worn a helmet, you idiot.*

Finally I arrived at the water. I turned and hiked along the shore until I found the dock. The rowboat was there, too, pitching up and down on the waves. Behind me, the sky was turning black.

Well, crap, I thought. *Things just got real.* All the way along, I'd expected to fail. I could barely see this morning, after all. I should never have got anywhere near this far.

There was another crack of thunder. An oily cloud blotted out the hills.

I stepped onto the dock and felt around for the rowboat's bowline. I untied it and thought: *Am I seriously going rowing in a thunderstorm?*

Yes I was. I most definitely was. I hadn't come this far to chicken out.

But what if lightning strikes? And what if the boat swamps? That lake is fed by melting glaciers. You could go hypothermic, even drown.

But this is probably my last chance to visit Perpetuum. And the floating island is my only way in.

I untied the stern line and stepped into the rowboat. *Last chance, Finn. Last chance to smarten up.*

I remembered that day at the jumping rocks. Tab shouting: "Don't think, Finn. Just jump!" It was good advice. I shoved off from the dock.

It started to rain. Wait a second; that was hail. Instantly, the lake went white with boiling ice.

96,815.

96,814.

I rowed that boat into the storm. The sky was grey-black and I had no idea where I was going. Freezing water sloshed over the sides of the boat. Where was the island? Where was the flashing blue light?

I pulled the straps on my life jacket tighter and wondered what Cheese and Tab were doing. I felt like a jerk for ditching them like this, but I'd never really expected to reach the rowboat.

The hail came down harder. It lashed my face and left welts on my arms. My whole body was shivering, and water kept pouring over the transom. I pulled at the oars, but I was barely making any progress. With all that water in the boat, it might as well have been filled with cement. *Am I actually going to sink?* I wondered. *If so, which way do I swim? I can't see the shore.*

I stopped rowing and looked around. Everything looked dark grey, except for the water and shoreline. They looked as black as I felt. And that was very black.

Silently, I composed one final list.

Why the World Will Be Better Off Without Me:
–I'm going blind and am therefore useless
–I only think of myself
–I'm unfunny, ungenerous, basically "un"
–I treat my parents like crap
–I treat my friends like crap, too

Take Cheese. I'd been a total jerk to him. He'd been bullied a lot last year, and I hadn't done much to stop it.

Then there were my parents. My sad, don't-know-what-to-do-about-me parents. They hadn't asked for this problem. They deserved a fully sighted son. One who wasn't blowing up in their faces all the time.

Maybe . . . maybe they *would* all be happier without me.

More water poured over the transom. It flooded the hull and sloshed around my calves. The hail changed to heavy rain; the kind that washes out roads and causes landslides.

No way could the island survive this pounding, I thought.

The hail turned to rain. The raindrops flashed like pieces of blue glass.

Three seconds later, I saw more blue.

Flickering. Flashing. Glimmering blue.

I dropped the oars and swung around. Saw a ghostly outline. Two trees and a ripsaw line of blue current.

I didn't think I had any energy left, but I suddenly grabbed the oars and yanked them through the water. The island was 5 metres away, then 3, then 1. The rowboat slid up against the island's side and stopped.

I sprang to the bow and swung my butt over the gunwale. I felt that familiar YANK, and once again I was falling. Falling away. Falling apart.

Somewhere behind me I heard a metallic *THWUPP* — the sound of zillions of seconds grinding to a halt.

CHAPTER
24

Blind Faith

Time remaining:
(centuries)

99
x 999
x 999,999
x 999,999,999
x 999,999,999,999
x 999,999,999,999,999
x 999,999,999,999,999,999
x 999,999,999,999,999,999,999
x 999,999,999,999,999,999,999,999
x 999,999,999,999,999,999,999,999,999
x 999,999,999,999,999,999,999,999,999,999
x 999,999,999,999,999,999,999,999,999,999,999
x 999,999,999,999,999,999,999,999,999,999,999,999
x 999,999,999,999,999,999,999,999,999,999,999,999,999
x 999,999,999,999,999,999,999,999,999,999,999,999,999,999
x 999,999,999,999,999,999,999,999,999,999,999,999,999,999,999
x 999,999,999,999,999,999,999,999,999,999,999,999,999,999,999,999
x 999,999,999,999,999,999,999,999,999,999,999,999,999,999,999,999,999
x 999,999,999,999,999,999,999,999,999,999,999,999,999,999,999,999,999,999
x 999,999,999,999,999,999,999,999,999,999,999,999,999,999,999,999,999,999,999
x 999,999,999,999,999,999,999,999,999,999,999,999,999,999,999,999,999,999,999,999
x 999,999,999,999,999,999,999,999,999,999,999,999,999,999,999,999,999,999,999,999,999
x 999,999,999,999,999,999,999,999,999,999,999,999,999,999,999,999,999,999,999,999,999,999

et cetera

"Come on, kiddo, you can *do* this!" Constant clapped her hands at the bottom of the jump.

It was my third attempt at a barspin.

The first two hadn't gone very well. I'd crashed both times, and yes, there was pain, but as Constant had promised, I didn't break my bones.

"What are you afraid of?" she shouted. "You can't die out here, remember?"

Maybe not, but barspins were surprisingly hard. If your front wheel wasn't perfectly straight when you landed, you'd jackknife sideways, usually straight into a tree.

"Come on!" Constant shouted. "Make me proud!"

I looked at the track on the far side of the jump. It was surrounded — on all sides — by trees.

"Go, Finn, go!" Constant shouted.

I rolled my shoulders and took a deep breath.

3, 2, 1 — go!

I started up the track. It was only 20 metres long, so I had to crank it hard to get the speed I needed.

"You own this!" Constant yelled.

The suspension compressed when I hit the jump. I threw my weight forward and kept my eyes locked straight ahead.

FWISSSSSS!

Liftoff. We have liftoff.

Welcome aboard FinnAir, flight 002, bound for the decline ramp and hopefully no trees. Estimated flying time: 1.2 seconds. Please enjoy our extensive on-board entertainment system . . .

I got a clean launch and rose into the air. I didn't get much pop, but my angle was pretty good. I pinched the seat between my lower legs and threw the handlebars with my right hand. The bike stayed straight and I caught the handlebars with my left. Then the wheels were back down and the flight was over.

"Nice one!" I heard Constant shout.

I came in a bit nose heavy and nearly got blown off the pedals, but somehow my skeletal system remained intact.

I hit the brakes and yanked off my brain-basket.

"You totally nailed it!" Constant cried.

I jumped off the bike and knelt down to check the pedals. A few pins were broken, but that was okay, I had extras.

"You'll be doing a Superman no-hander before you know it," Constant said.

"Ha," I said. "Only the superstars do that move."

"You're a superstar," said Constant. "Well, to me you are, anyway." She put me in a headlock and ruffled my hair.

"I'll be lucky if I ever master a bike whip," I said.

"You will," said Constant. "You've got lots of time, remember?"

Yeah, yeah, so I've been told.

I walked the bike away from the jump line. The chain clicked softly as it rolled over the new cassette. The bike was riding more smoothly than ever, thanks to the new components I'd found in the fields. The bike had front- and rear-wheel suspension now, and some SRAM XO components. All I needed was a better frame — a Pivot Mach 6 or something like that. Then I could do some *really* good tricks.

For a moment, I wished Cheese and Tab had seen me nail that barspin. Then I caught myself and thought: *Easy, don't think about them.*

"Hey, how's your research coming?" I asked Constant.

She was wearing baggy boy jeans with rips in the knees and scuffed-up Doc Martens boots. She had on a Saskatchewan Rough Riders toque. It sat at the back of her hair like a tattered, green bird's nest.

"I've actually put that stuff on hold," she said.

"How come?" I said. "Have you given up?"

"Not exactly," she said. "I'm just focusing on other things. You know how you've got three or four projects on the go? The bike tricks, your guitar lessons and that new drop line you're building? I think that's a smart way to go. When you get bored of one thing, you move on to another. That's what I'm doing with my research. I just need a break."

"But I thought you were making headway."

She sighed. "I thought so, too, but now I wonder. I found patterns in the data that pointed in one direction, but I couldn't find anything to prove my theory. If I could run some tests, I think I could find corroborating evidence. But I don't have the equipment — or the people — to do the testing. So I'm stuck."

"You said, uh, that you found patterns in the data. What kind of patterns are we talking about?"

She sighed and adjusted her toque. "It's complicated," she said. "If I could just talk to some research scientists, run my ideas past them, then they could swat me down and explain to me why my theory's crazy. I'd love that. Then at least I could move on to something else."

"But what if they didn't swat you down?" I asked. "What if they decided your theory made sense?"

Constant waved that off. "Won't happen," she said. "It would be lovely if it did, but it's impossible. I'm self-taught, remember?"

I spun the crank and the pedal rotated. Something had become clear to me while she was speaking. "You really need to go back," I said, getting to my feet.

"Go back where?" she said.

"Back home," I said. "You could talk to some scientists. I don't see what's stopping you."

"A spare Glimmer Line is what's stopping me," Constant said.

"Take mine," I said. "It's just sitting there empty. It's right over those hills." I pointed.

Constant shook her head. "Can't," she said. "I won't strand you here."

"How do you know I'll be stranded?" I asked.

"Because the only thing I can deduce about Glimmer Lines is that they work on the basis of one person in, one person out."

I looked at Constant in that ridiculous toque. "How do you know that for sure?" I asked. "You said you *thought* they worked like that."

She picked up a clump of dirt and tossed it toward the ravine. "Because I tried your Glimmer Line once," she said.

What?

"Remember the last time you went back?" she explained. "You got into the rowboat with your friends. I followed you out there and watched you step through. Then I tried to step through, too."

"What happened?" I asked.

"It was like walking into a wall. So you see? One person in, one person out."

Aha. I knew it. She'd wanted out.

"You need to go back," I said. "For your daughter's sake."

"Stop saying that," she said. "I'm not going anywhere."

"Your research might help save her life," I said. "Who knows, it could maybe save lots of lives."

Constant rolled her eyes.

"Okay," I said. "So maybe you haven't invented a cure. But who knows? Maybe your ideas will help some other scientist, and together the two of you will . . . "

Now Constant's eyes were spinning drill bits. "Listen to me, Finn," she said. "As long as I stay here, I know my daughter is alive. But the moment I go back, my clock starts ticking again, and then . . . "

"And then what?" I said.

"Then there's no guarantee, is there?"

Constant clutched her hair and frizzed it up.

"But what if Rowyn survives?" I shouted. "You keep talking like she's going to die, but what if she lives? Do you want her to grow up without her mother?"

Constant bit her lip and hung her head on an angle. I suddenly felt ashamed, like I'd accidentally set a house on fire.

"I'm really sorry," I said. "That was mean, I shouldn't have — "

"It's okay," she said quietly.

"It's just that, I've got lots of projects to keep me busy. If you wanted to borrow my Glimmer Line, even for a little while, I wouldn't mind."

"I thought you were getting sick of the school work," Constant said. "Remember when you said you wanted to quit?"

True. I did want to quit sometimes. Especially grade eleven biology.

Nucleus, mitochondria, cytoplasm, ribosomes, endo-plasmic reticulum — My forehead went *clunk* against the table.

This was three or four days earlier. Correction: not days. More like *un-days*.

"I know it's not very exciting," Constant had said. "But you need to understand the life sciences first."

"I know," I'd sighed. "But why does it have to be so dull?"

She'd looked out the window of the tree house, combing the fields for "new arrivals." Then she'd walked over to the bookshelf and started thumbing through the textbooks, giving me a pep talk all the while.

"Just do a little bit at a time," she said. "Remember, you've chosen a long-term project."

Right. I needed to pace myself. It wasn't as if I had a tight deadline or anything.

"How long do you think it'll take me?" I asked.

Constant pulled out an old atlas and then shoved it back in. "Well, you need your high school equivalency, and four years of pre-med studies. Then medical school and graduate school. After that, you should specialize for a couple of years. By then you should have enough general knowledge to — pardon the pun — *focus* on your research."

She grinned at me from under that toque. Then her smile faded, as if she'd remembered something sad.

"I know it sounds like a lot," she said. "But you can take breaks. You could even go home if you want, and then come back."

I shut my biology textbook. Going home wasn't part of the plan.

"Don't you ever miss your parents?" Constant had asked.

Seriously? Do we really have to talk about this?

"I try not to think about them too much," I said.

Constant's cheek twitched, and she looked back toward the window. "What about your friends?"

When I first arrived, I'd thought about Cheese and Tab all the time. I worried about what they'd think of me when they noticed I was gone. I had to keep reminding myself that time wasn't passing for them. Cheese was still lying in the hammock. Tab was still chasing after Skyforce.

Actually, no. The storm would have driven them inside while I was heading for the island. Still, time wasn't passing for them the way it was here. Cheese might have noticed that I was missing, but he sure wouldn't be worried. Not yet.

Still, I missed the two of them — and even my parents — sometimes. When I thought about their faces, my feelings could get pretty swampy. So I eventually decided to stop thinking about them altogether. Whenever their faces came into my mind, I just changed the channel.

Maybe one day I'll want to go back and see them, I thought. *But not now. There isn't anything there for me anymore.*

One of Constant's bootlaces had come loose. She knelt down to retie it. "Remind me what you're doing out here," she said.

"I already told you," I said. "I want to find a cure for Stargardt disease."

She nodded and retied the other lace, even though it hadn't come loose. When she finished, she stood back up. "I don't believe you," she said.

I looked out from the tree house. The sky looked washed out, as usual.

"Don't get me wrong," she had said. "I love that you're here. I don't know how I ever managed before you arrived. But you shouldn't be here. You've got your whole life ahead of you. A real life, with real family, real friends."

"Not to mention real blindness," I added.

"*Legal* blindness," she corrected me. "You'll always have peripheral vision. You probably won't even need a cane."

"And here I've got perfect vision, awesome bike trails, no school, plus I can drive a truck anytime I want. And look for a cure . . . "

"That's not why you're really here," Constant said. "That's just a convenient excuse."

"Oh yeah? So why am I here?"

"Because you're scared. That's why we're both here."

Her head tilted down, as if she was ashamed by what she'd said. She licked her finger and rubbed a scuff mark off her boot.

"Remember that time you didn't want me to leave?" I said. "You kept talking about how awful the world is."

"I did that?" Constant said.

"Yeah. You talked about all the poverty and disease out there."

Constant smirked and picked at the toe of her boot. "I was probably scared that you'd go home and learn the truth."

"What truth is that?" I asked.

Constant raised her head. Her green eyes looked cloudy. "That there's more good stuff in the world than bad," she said. "It just depends on what you choose to see."

Later, I realized that she was talking more to herself than to me. Convincing herself that it was okay to go home.

Eventually Constant agreed to use my Glimmer Line, though she insisted that she was only leaving on a temporary basis. She promised to come back, right after she'd spent some time with her family and delivered the research she'd collected to a university in England.

"You're sure you're okay with this?" she asked.

Yeah, I thought. *I'm okay. I'll be lonely, I guess. But I'm used to being alone.*

"I really promise to come back," she said.

I remembered what she'd said before; about how I shouldn't trust her, and how you should never underestimate a mother's love for her child. A part of me almost hoped that she wouldn't return — that she'd stay and be a mom to her sick, little girl.

"Stay as long as you want," I said. "I already told you. I'm happy here."

We hiked over the purple hills together, and she took my arm as we strolled through the cornfield. Walking with her reminded me of my grade six grad, when all the guys got escorted onto the stage by their moms.

Soon we came to the end of the cornfield. Two trees stood like sentinels above us. We climbed a little rise and stepped between the trees, and suddenly a black lake spread out in front of us. The sky was dark with flying rain, but the raindrops weren't moving; they just floated in mid-air. Off in the distance, I could see high cliffs along the shore. *That's Alberta,* I reminded myself. It looked like a strip of grey gauze.

"Remember any of this?" she asked me.

I nodded. "It's my Glimmer Line."

Cables of tree roots snaked across the ground and a dazzling blue line scored the water's edge.

Constant pointed at a wooden rowboat. "Is that your ride?"

I nodded. It was half-full of water. The bow had crossed over the Glimmer Line. The stern had not.

"You said you wore a life jacket," Constant said.

"I did," I said.

"Good." Constant looked relieved. "Where is it?"

"Right there."

I pointed at the birch tree behind us. I'd slung the life jacket over one of its branches.

Constant's face turned to ash.

"What's wrong?" I asked.

"You should've left it in the boat," she said.

I stared at the life jacket. Then I turned back to Constant. She was hunched over; she looked broken.

"What are you talking about?" I said.

"Don't you remember?"

I struggled to recall what had happened when I'd arrived. The icy water had been gushing over the stern, so I'd leapt to the bow and jumped over the gunwale without thinking. I was only trying to get to safety. I was only trying to keep from going in the drink . . .

Suddenly it hit me. I'd worn it in.

You can bring things in, but you can't always take them out.

Oh, God. I'd brought the life jacket in. Which meant it might not get back *out*.

"Hang on," I said. "I got my phone out once before. And my clothes always get out fine. Does a life jacket count as clothes?"

Constant shrugged her shoulders. "Doubt it," she said. "I

wore a necklace the first time I came. It never got out. I haven't seen it since."

I looked down at the swamped rowboat. Then I looked up. The lake was ribbed with long metal waves that had foamy egg whites riding on their backs.

We weren't even 500 metres from shore. That wasn't far for a good swimmer. But in this storm? Through those waves? In ice-cold water? Without a life jacket? No way.

"How strong a swimmer are you?" I asked Constant.

No reply. She was staring down the lake.

"It . . . " She squinted and took a deep breath. "It doesn't matter," she said, shaking her head.

"What do you mean?" I asked.

She stepped even closer to the water's edge. She was less than a metre from the Glimmer Line now.

"Look over there."

I followed her gaze to a strange bulge in the lake. Two little spheres were rising out of the water.

I squinted toward where she was looking.

"Is that who I think it is?" Constant asked.

I suddenly felt sick — like someone had forced a snake down my throat.

Cheese and Tab were clinging to an overturned canoe.

CHAPTER 25

Going Dark

Time remaining:
(millennia)

99
x 999
x 999,999
x 999,999,999
x 999,999,999,999
x 999,999,999,999,999
x 999,999,999,999,999,999
x 999,999,999,999,999,999,999
x 999,999,999,999,999,999,999,999
x 999,999,999,999,999,999,999,999,999
x 999,999,999,999,999,999,999,999,999,999
x 999,999,999,999,999,999,999,999,999,999,999
x 999,999,999,999,999,999,999,999,999,999,999,999
x 999,999,999,999,999,999,999,999,999,999,999,999,999
x 999,999,999,999,999,999,999,999,999,999,999,999,999,999
x 999,999,999,999,999,999,999,999,999,999,999,999,999,999,999
x 999,999,999,999,999,999,999,999,999,999,999,999,999,999,999,999
x 999,999,999,999,999,999,999,999,999,999,999,999,999,999,999,999,999
x 999,999,999,999,999,999,999,999,999,999,999,999,999,999,999,999,999,999
x 999,999,999,999,999,999,999,999,999,999,999,999,999,999,999,999,999,999,999
x 999,999,999,999,999,999,999,999,999,999,999,999,999,999,999,999,999,999,999,999
x 999,999,999,999,999,999,999,999,999,999,999,999,999,999,999,999,999,999,999,999,999
x 999,999,999,999,999,999,999,999,999,999,999,999,999,999,999,999,999,999,999,999,999,999
x 999,999,999,999,999,999,999,999,999,999,999,999,999,999,999,999,999,999,999,999,999,999,999
x 999,999,999,999,999,999,999,999,999,999,999,999,999,999,999,999,999,999,999,999,999,999,999,999

et cetera

In a heartbeat, the fog of forgetfulness lifted. Now that I could see my friends, I remembered why I loved them.

Cheese's *winning ideas.*

Tab speaking Portuguese.

Cheese Hula Hooping to Mozart.

Tab's hand on mine.

It all came flooding back in a heartbeat. Cheese's weird vocabulary and fashion sense. Tab's fearlessness at the jumping rocks.

Pooched. That's what they were. Pooched. Their canoe had gone turtle. It looked like they were kicking their way to shore.

Idiots! You don't go canoeing in a thunderstorm. Especially not in a glacier-fed lake. Even if they could kick that canoe to shore, they'd never do it before hypothermia set in.

"How cold is that water?" Constant asked.

"Ice cold," I said. "It comes from glaciers."

How had Cheese and Tab known I was here? Had Tab spotted me when I ran into Skyforce? Must have. But how did Cheese get out here? When I'd left Splitsville, he was still reading a book in the hammock.

Somehow they'd figured out where I'd gone. And then they'd chased me up the Organ Donor — carrying the *canoe.* But why had they bothered? I wasn't worth it. Surely Tab knew that. Especially after all that stuff I said in my bedroom.

Message to Cheese: *I don't need saving.*

Message to Tab: *What were you thinking? Those waves are huge.*

Stupid, stupid, stupid, I thought. *Are they trying to get themselves killed?*

Crap. Only a minute ago, I'd known what I wanted. I wanted

Constant to go home and be a mother to her daughter. Now I wanted the opposite thing. I wanted to dive into the water and save my best friends.

I looked at the sky. It was really amazing. Veins of lightning were glowing inside the bellies of the clouds.

"If this rowboat sinks," Constant said, "and there's a good chance it will, whoever's in it will need to swim."

I looked back down. The gunwales were above water, but barely.

I looked back at the trees. They were bent in the wind.

"How good a swimmer are you?" I asked Constant.

"Not very," she said, looking at the rowboat.

"Did you earn any swimming badges?" I asked.

She smirked. "I got one that had some kind of fish on it."

"Was it the dolphin badge?" I asked. "Or the guppy?"

"I can't remember," said Constant. "I knew how to bob, and I could do the flutter kick, but that's about all." She walked over to the tree and lifted the life jacket down. "I know what'll happen if that boat sinks. I'll hit that water and then I'll start to panic. I'm telling you, I know my limits. I don't stand a chance of saving your friends."

She held the life jacket out to me. I shook my head. "You're still a better bet than me," I said. "At least you can see where you're going."

"Don't do that," Constant shot back. "Don't use your eyes as an *excuse*."

Stop the clock. What did she just say?

"Vision is just one way of seeing," she said. "There are plenty of others. Pay attention."

I looked back at Cheese and Tab. *You guys,* I thought. *What the heck were you thinking?* How long had they been in that water? Might've been 10 seconds; might've been 10 minutes.

"You have to try," I said to Constant. "Do it for your daughter. And your research."

She pulled out a Ziploc bag and folded it into quarters.

"What's that?" I asked.

"The research," she said.

She tucked it into my pants pocket.

"But what if this doesn't get out?" I said.

"Clothes get out, right? And this'll be *inside* your clothes."

"Your necklace didn't get out. There's no guarantee this'll work," I said.

"I know," said Constant. "But it's our best shot. If it gets through, please deliver it to Dr. Victoria Sanita at the Brownridge Institute in England."

"Okay," I said.

"Repeat her name."

I repeated it.

Constant looked into my eyes. "I'm sorry," she said. "This isn't what either of us wanted."

She pulled the life jacket over my shoulders and zipped it up. "This probably won't go through either, but it's worth a try." She tightened the drawstring and then stood back and looked me over. "The moment you get into that boat, start bailing," she said. "Stay in the bow, so the stern won't go under."

I looked at her face. Strands of hair had come loose. I thought of her sitting in the tree house without me.

"Fling the water out, as fast as you can," she said. "Then, start rowing like hell."

I pictured her doing her research all alone. Doing magic

tricks, all alone. Sitting in the pickup truck — alone.

"You have to try to get out," I said. "Promise me you'll get out."

Constant smiled. "Oh, don't worry about me. I'll get out somehow. I've got plenty of time, remember?"

I tried to smile, but my face muscles weren't working. Her smile disappeared, too.

"Try to bring the bike with you when you come," I said.

"I'll do my best," she said.

"The guitar, too. I love that guitar."

She put her hands on my shoulders and turned me around. "Now go," she said. "Before I kick you out."

I took a deep breath and stepped over the gunwale — and over the Glimmer Line, too. I heard the familiar *fffft* sound, and then the roar of the storm, and suddenly the rain and wind were blasting my chest. Instantly I lost balance and toppled sideways, right into the lake.

CHAPTER
26

Sight Unseen

Okay, hitting that water hurt.

Hurt a *lot*.

The cold didn't just take my breath away. It took my brain away. It took my reason to live away.

My heart screamed and I couldn't get any air. *Constant! What the* bleep *just happened?*

A bad start; that's what happened. I hadn't expected the wind to be so fierce.

Now the world was a liquid, grey-black smear. I reached up and grabbed the side of the boat. I just clung there for a moment, trying to catch my breath. My muscles clamped up like a twisted bike chain. My arms and legs felt like slabs of cement.

I noticed that I wasn't wearing a life jacket. That meant something bad, but for a minute I couldn't remember what it was. Had the water been this cold when Cheese pulled me from Drag River? Nope, it must've been colder. There was ice on that river. Right.

Breathe steady, Finn. In and out.

Better. Now, get yourself into that rowboat.

I worked my way along to the bow and pulled myself up. My weight pushed the bow down, and the water in the stern spilled forward. That pushed the bow down even farther and I slipped aboard like a seal. There! I was in.

I moved back to the middle seat and grabbed the bailer. Then, as fast as I could, I flung water over the side.

Faster! Cheese and Tab need your help. You left Perpetuum for this. Constant stayed behind so you could get out. Make it count!

The icy water sloshed against my shins, jolting me with its toe-clenching voltage. I looked back at Perpetuum, hoping to see Constant. But the rain was blinding. I couldn't even see the trees.

"Constant!" I howled. "Where are you?"

The wind roared back. Nothing else.

"Come on!" I shouted. "Try the Glimmer Line! If you can hear me, try it now!"

There was no response — except for the wind. Constant must've been right. Glimmer Lines only worked for one.

I kept bailing and shouting for Constant, even though I knew she couldn't hear me. I'd already been in the boat for a couple of minutes. Which was who knows how long on Perpetuum. Decades? Centuries?

Once I'd shovelled most of the water out of the boat, I slammed the oars into the oarlocks. I pulled forward on one and reversed with the other. The boat swung 180 degrees.

Now ROW, I told myself. *Hard as you can!*

I started pulling at the oars, but then I stopped. *How do I know if I'm going the right way?*

Calm down, I told myself. *Remember what Constant said.*

Vision is just one way of seeing. There are others. Pay attention.

I grabbed the oars and pretended they were bike pedals. I dug in as if I was riding the relay at CrankWorx.

"Cheese! Tab! Where are you? Talk to me!"

The rowboat bashed through the waves like a battering ram.

CHAPTER 27

The Blind Card

Geysers of spray exploded over the bow. I had no way of knowing if I was going the right way or not. I just hoped to get close enough to hear Cheese and Tab shouting. If they were conscious, I was sure they'd call out.

"Tab! Cheese!"

Was that a shout? It sounded like something. But it was impossible to tell with the howling wind.

"Talk to me, guys! *Where are you?*"

Then, suddenly, distinctly: *"FINN!"*

I heard that for sure. A girl's voice. Close by.

"Where are you?" I shouted. "Keep yelling!"

"Over here! Hurry up!"

I rowed back and forth, like a zigzagging moth, trying to zero in on my target. There was a flash of lightning, and for a second I saw them. Two yellow blobs. Life jackets — off to the right.

I pulled at the oars, and the rowboat swung to starboard. The bow nose-dived under a wave, but then popped back up.

"Keep coming! Keep coming! A little more!"

A green ghost appeared to my right — the swamped

canoe. At either end, I saw the yellow blobs.

I grabbed the shoulder of one life jacket and hauled it into the rowboat. It was Tab. Her teeth were chattering so hard I could barely make out her words.

"Cheese needs help," she gasped.

I leapt to the stern and held out an oar to the other yellow blob. I felt pressure on the other end. He'd grabbed it, thank goodness.

"Don't worry," I shouted as I pulled him to the side of the boat.

"Finn?" he stuttered.

"You'll be fine," I said.

His face was bloodless white, like a winter moon. I reached down and pulled him up and over the gunwale. He lay down and rested his head on the hull. His body looked so small lying there.

"Which way?" I asked Tab.

She knelt beside me and pointed left. I started rowing again — hard.

The wind flung sheets of spray through the air. It felt like someone was emptying a staple gun in my face. From time to time I looked down at Cheese. He still hadn't said anything aside from my name.

How long until hypothermia sets in? Twenty minutes?

Don't think, Finn. Just row. Harder!

The waves were cold, grey guillotine blades.

"Doing good, Finn," Tab managed.

I was about to answer, but a flash of lightning and an almost instantaneous clap of thunder drowned out my words.

Wow. That was close. Directly above our heads.

"How much farther?" I shouted.

Tab said something I couldn't hear. Another wave crashed over us. I stabbed the oars back into the water. Raindrops shot through the air like bullets.

Crack!

Another lightning strike. So close the air concussion threw me back. Tab and I smacked heads with a sickening *clack*. For a moment, everything went silent and white.

"Ho-ly," said Cheese. He was sitting up.

"What?" I said. A high-pitched whistle rang in my ears.

Tab swung around. "That lightning hit the floating island," she said. "One of the trees is on fire. No, both of them are."

I didn't bother to look. I wouldn't have seen anything anyway. *Don't think, Finn. Just row.*

Tab was rubbing her head. "Listen — " she said.

I heard it, too. Waves crashing against a cliff. We must've been near the eastern shore of the lake.

"We need to go closer in," said Tab.

"But we'll get crushed," I said.

"Don't worry," said Tab. "I know where we're going."

Vision is just one way of seeing, Constant had said. *There are plenty of others. Pay attention.*

I had to trust Tab, even though it felt wrong. "Which way?" I shouted.

"Straight ahead. Keep going. Keep going!"

The wind blew harder and started whistling. The rain was turning back into hail. Suddenly we rose up on a wave and surged toward the cliff. "Now, Finn!" Tab yelled. "Row fast — RIGHT NOW!"

I pulled the oars up to my chest, then lifted them up and

pushed them away. Drop, deep pull, lift up and push away. The boat rose up on a wave and the wind caught us and we were surging. My face felt like a dartboard from the spray. We raced toward the cliff.

"Now backpaddle right!" Tab yelled. "BACKPADDLE RIGHT!"

I plunged the paddle into the water in mid-stroke and pushed it away from me as hard as I could.

"Easy!" Tab shouted. "Everyone hang on!"

The boat swung sideways and then — *CRUNCH*.

The wave dropped us onto a narrow shelf of rock.

"Ooof," Cheese grunted. "Smooth landing, Finn."

I grinned. I was happy to hear his voice.

"Come on!" Tab shouted. "Everyone out!"

She grabbed my arm and yanked me onto the rocky ledge just as another wave crashed against the cliff. When the water receded, she grabbed Cheese and pulled him onto the path in front of me.

"Follow me," she shouted. "And stay close."

"As if we had any choice," Cheese muttered.

Another wave swept over our legs. Behind us, I heard the rowboat grinding against the rocks.

"Whoa!" I said. "Blind guy back here, remember?"

Tab and Cheese had suddenly disappeared. I took a few steps forward and then I understood. There was a gap in the rock. They'd gone into a narrow cave.

The moment I rounded the corner and stepped into the crevasse, the wind dropped away. My core muscles relaxed, and for the first time in what seemed like ages, I took a deep breath.

"Squeeze in tight," said Tab, unclipping and peeling off her life vest. "This storm can't last forever."

Grimy light drifted down from above and painted a grey slash on the floor of the cave. The ground was littered with broken slabs of shale that clinked like pieces of shattered china when we walked. Water trickled down the walls of the crevasse, which soared up on both sides like a stone cathedral.

I took one last look out at the lake — not that I could make out very much. It was like trying to see through the windshield in a carwash. I hugged myself for warmth and stomped my feet against the ground.

"Everyone do jumping jacks," Tab said. "We need to keep warm. Keep the blood pumping."

"I'm too tired," Cheese muttered.

"You're in shock," said Tab, wringing water out of her T-shirt. "We all are, probably. Come on, everybody jump."

The rock walls flashed yellow. There was a far-off crash of thunder, and a stream of small rocks clattered down on our heads as we jumped.

"What's happening with the island?" Cheese asked, his teeth chattering.

"Good question," said Tab. She made her way down to the mouth of the cave. "It's hard to see much through the rain, but the trees are still burning," she called back. "They're farther apart than they should be. Maybe the island's breaking up?"

It's over, I thought. *My doorway to Perpetuum is gone.*

The thought made me sick.

"One tree just fell over," said Tab. "The taller one."

I could imagine it keeling over, slowly but surely, until the flames on the branches were snuffed out by the lake.

"There goes the second one," Tab said a moment later. "The island's breaking up. I can make out two separate chunks."

Oh, God, I thought. *The island really is going. I've lost my way back forever. The ability to drive a car. Ride a bike. Hang out with Constant. Find a cure for Stargardt. All gone. And Constant . . .*

A blast of wind shrieked through the cave. Cheese did a few more jumping jacks and then stopped.

"Why don't we just walk home?" I said.

"Not while there's lightning," said Tab. "We've taken enough risks already."

Her teeth were chattering, too. She stuffed her hands into her armpits.

"What was all that about anyway, Finn?" she asked. "You could've gotten yourself killed, taking off like that."

"I didn't ask you to follow me," I said.

"Right," said Cheese. "We were just going to let you commit hara-kiri."

"It wasn't hara-kiri," I said. "I was trying to do you guys a favour."

More lightning. Then, a few seconds later, thunder. The storm was finally moving away. "How did you guys even know I was here?" I asked. "You're supposed to be back in Splitsville, Cheese."

"I wish I was," said Cheese. "Unfortunately, your parents discovered you were missing, and I got sucked into this elaborate plot to save your life."

"That's right!" said Tab, putting a hand on Cheese's arm. "Finn still doesn't know . . . "

"Know what?" I said.

"Your parents had this whole big plan," Cheese went on. "They were going to take us over to the Coleys' place in the motorboat."

"I called you this morning," said Tab. "But you were asleep, and Cheese said you were all going back to the city, and then my mom got involved . . . "

"Of course everything changed when we discovered you were missing," Cheese said. "Your parents flipped out, and that sort of sped everything up."

What the heck are they talking about?

"That reminds me," said Tab. She pulled out her phone.

"Texting our coordinates to the parentals?" Cheese asked.

"Yeah," said Tab. "Except — oh, crap — it's totally dead. It went swimming, remember?" She shook it and wiped it on her shorts.

"Try mine," said Cheese.

"It went swimming, too," said Tab.

"Yeah, but it was in a Ziploc bag."

Suddenly I remembered — Constant's research! I jammed my hands into my pockets. Turned them inside out. Nothing there. Tried the pockets again. Still nothing.

You can take things in, but you can't always take them out. Had I lost the notes when I'd landed in the water, or had they even made it that far? Constant . . .

Cheese passed his phone to Tab. "Any reception?" he asked.

"It's spotty, but yeah, I think it'll work."

She tapped away on the phone.

"Anyway," Cheese went on. "First your parents and I went to Tab's place. Then we split up to look for you. Your parents headed back out in the motorboat, looking along the shoreline. But Tab thought you might be heading here."

"We had to keep that part secret," said Tab. "They were all freaking out about you being missing. They thought they might be looking for your washed-up *body*. They never would've let us go paddling if we'd asked. So we had to sneak the canoe out from under their noses."

Oh, God. I put my head in my hands. "I'm so sorry," I said. "I was just trying to do the right thing . . . "

Tab gave the phone back to Cheese. "I got through," she said. "I told them where we are."

Everything felt black. I wondered why I'd left Perpetuum at all. Then I remembered. To save my friends.

You chose this, I told myself. *And you made the right choice.*

"You guys must really hate me," I muttered.

"Why would we hate you?" Tab asked.

They stared at me.

"Because of what I said last night," I said, looking at Tab. "I really am a freak show. On account of my anxiety, and, you know, *my eyes.*"

Tab shook her head. "Finn, don't you *get* it? If you were a jerk, then we might hate you. But blindness?"

"Give us just a tiny bit of credit," said Cheese.

I felt like I was on a swaying ship. Also — an express elevator going down. I was on a swaying ship, falling down an elevator shaft. That's approximately what it felt like. Plus, I was freezing cold.

"A disability isn't enough to scare us off," said Tab. "You can do lots of what we can. You just need some help."

Easy for you to say, I thought. *You're not the one asking for help.*

"But what if I don't want help?" I said. "What if I want to be normal like you?"

"Us? Normal?" said Cheese. "That's a joke."

Just then a clap of thunder made Cheese's words sound profound. The three of us laughed.

"I like doing stuff on my own," I said. "But now if I want to go biking, I have to find someone with a tandem bike. If I want to go to the mall, I have to get someone to drive me. Or I have to take the bus, which royally sucks — Wait a second . . . "

I stopped talking. Cheese had taken off his shoes. His feet were as yellow as Brazil's soccer jersey.

"What's wrong with your feet?" I said.

"I'm not sure," he said. "I can't feel them."

"Wiggle your toes," said Tab.

"I'm trying," said Cheese.

This is stupid, I thought. *All this body heat going to waste. Do I really have to be the one to say it?*

Yes, Finn, you do. You left Perpetuum to help them. Finish the job. Do the scary thing.

"I totally get it if you guys don't want to," I said. "But we'd stay warmer if we all, just . . . you know . . . hugged."

Tab pulled her hair over her shoulder and wrung it out. She shrugged. "The boy's right. Come on, Cheese. Group hug."

We sat down in a knot and huddled together, foreheads touching. Cheese wrapped his arms around me and Tab, while we rubbed his feet with our hands.

"Finn? You okay?" said Tab.

No, not really.

"It's okay, buddy," said Cheese. "Let it out. We're all friends here."

When he said that, I started shivering again, but not the kind of shivering that comes from being cold. It was a different kind of shiver, the emotional kind, and I wished the thunder would come again so we could all just laugh, but it didn't.

"Hey, Cheese! Hug him tighter," said Tab.

They pressed their bodies closer against mine. I was shaking uncontrollably. "I'm sorry," I gasped. "I'm so sorry."

"That's okay," said Cheese. "You saved our lives."

"No I didn't," I said. "You were only there because of me."

"Okay, so then we're even," said Cheese.

"Tighter, Cheese!" said Tab.

They squeezed me tighter and tighter, and then someone started to laugh and then we were all laughing, and my waterworks weren't so obvious.

"You're the real lifesaver," I told Cheese. "Which reminds me, why didn't you tell Tab you pulled me out of that river?"

He coughed a couple of times. His feet were still cold in my hands. "It just seemed like a private thing," he muttered. "Besides, I didn't do anything special. Anybody else would've done the same thing."

Did he really believe that? That just anybody would run into a frozen river? No way. Cheese was one in a thousand.

"Plus," he went on, "my parents taught me not to be a braggart."

"Oh, really?" said Tab. "They don't want you to be a *braggart*?" She rubbed Cheese's hair. He rubbed hers back.

"Everyone brags," I said. "I would've bragged my head off if I'd saved your life."

For a moment, Cheese didn't say anything. Then he looked at me and said, "That's really funny."

"How come?" I said.

"Because you *did* save my life."

What was he talking about?

"You obviously didn't even notice," said Cheese. "I didn't get beat up once last term. That's because of you. Because we're friends."

"But I didn't really *do* anything," I said.

"Remember first term?" Cheese said. "Some kids wrote *terrorist* on my locker, just because of where my parents are from. That all stopped after you and I started hanging out."

Suddenly I felt incredibly tired, more tired than I'd ever been in my life. I felt my breath coming easier, and feeling was coming back into my fingers.

"You may find this hard to believe," said Cheese. "But you've actually been a pretty good friend. Yes, you can be a jerk from time to time, and the panic attacks are intense, but aside from that, you're okay."

Cheese's phone vibrated. He pulled it out of his pocket. The light from the screen made his face glow blue.

"They're close," he said. "They want to meet us at the Organ Donor."

"Perfect," said Tab. "And the storm is calming down. I think this cave has a back entrance. There's light up there, see?"

Cheese must've sensed my confusion, because he said, "You might want to figure out your story. Your parents will want to know what was going on."

"Just tell them you got lost," said Tab. "You were looking for my place, but you stumbled around and got totally lost."

"Yeah, play the blind card," said Cheese. "No point

mentioning the floating island. They'll just think you're going crazy."

Tab gave me a nudge when he said that. I couldn't help but laugh.

"If I had bad vision, I'd play the blind card all the time," Cheese said. "Sorry, Mom, I had no idea my room was so messy . . . Sorry about missing curfew, Dad, I just misread the clock."

They were right. There are plenty of downsides to having bad vision. The blind card is a rare upside. Might as well use it.

We stood and started walking up the narrow cave. I held my hands out in front of my face so I wouldn't whack into any rocks. "What I still don't get," I said, "is why my parents went to see your parents in the first place."

Instantly, I saw the flash of Tab's teeth. "Oh, right," she said. "We forgot to tell you."

"Tell me what?" I said.

"The good news," said Cheese.

"You're not going back to the city yet," said Tab. "You guys get to stay with me."

CHAPTER
28

The Visionary

Seconds until departure: 518,400
Seconds until Lights Out: 140,032,800

I awoke to a smelly foot in my face.

What the?

I pushed the foot away and threw back the blankets. Rubbed the eye snot out of the corners of my eyes.

The pine walls were filled, floor to ceiling, with bookshelves, and sunshine was pouring through the window. None of it made sense until I saw, amid a tangle of blankets, Cheese's arms and legs.

Right, I thought. *It's Thursday morning. Tab's cabin.*

I grabbed my phone off the nightstand and checked the time. Then I did a quick calculation. *Doot, doot, doot.* 518,400 seconds left until we went home.

I did another calculation. The Lights Out number. My stomach lurched. In a few hours that big number — 140 million — would drop by one million, down to 139 million.

That happened every twelve days. Every twelve days, we all lose a million seconds of our lives. For me, that felt like I'd lost 1/140th of my remaining sight. It was a sickening feeling, but I was getting used to it — sort of.

I stood up, put on the sunglasses Tab's dad had lent me and wrapped a blanket around my shoulders. Then I padded down the hallway to the kitchen. I stared out the picture window at the explosion of colour. Purple clouds moved slowly across the sky. Wet pine branches gleamed like shiny grapes.

I opened the fridge and grabbed a tub of yogourt, carried it to the island and spooned myself a bowl. Normally I wouldn't eat someone else's food without asking, but nobody was awake yet, and I was pretty hungry.

"Oink," said a voice behind me.

Tab. Wearing a T-shirt the length of Saskatchewan.

"Sour cream for breakfast?" she asked.

"This isn't yogourt?"

"No."

"Oh — thanks."

I was finding it tricky, staying at someone else's house. Everything was in a different place from what I was used to. I spooned the sour cream back into the tub while Tab grabbed a different container from the fridge.

"Did I tell you that I once mistook my dad's foot cream for toothpaste?" I asked Tab.

"Ew. Gross."

She handed me the yogourt and grabbed a banana out of the fruit bowl, then peeled it and cut it into slices.

"Another time I had chapped lips," I said, "so I put on what I thought was lip balm. It wasn't. It was my mom's lipstick. Of course, I didn't find that out until I was on the bus."

Tab snorted and pulled up a second stool. Yellow light danced on the walls behind her.

"Sleep okay?" she asked.

"Three out of ten."

"Nightmares?"

"No, just couldn't sleep."

She poured some cereal into a bowl.

"I keep thinking about Constant," I said. "All her research, gone to waste."

"Maybe she found another way out," said Tab. "Maybe she found another Glimmer Line or something."

"I hope so," I said. "She sounded pretty confident she'd get out. Like it was just a matter of time — and she's got tons of that. It's just really brutal to think that — "

I stopped talking. "Wait a second. You *believe me*?"

Tab resealed the granola box. "I'm not saying that I believe everything *completely*." She smiled. "But the circumstantial evidence is adding up. I'm trying to keep an open mind."

Cheese must've talked to her, I thought. *Tried to convince her that I wasn't losing my marbles.*

"I can show you some more magic tricks if you want," I said.

"Don't push it," said Tab.

" . . . or we could have another conversation in Spanish."

That smile again. She brushed her hair off her shoulder.

"Let's just say, I'm open to the idea," she said.

Skyforce barked somewhere outside the cabin.

"But I still think you should talk to someone," she said. "Whether it's a therapist or your parents, or even me."

I grabbed the orange juice carton and poured myself a glass. "Fair enough," I said. "I can do that."

Tab offered me some banana, and I dropped the slices into my yogourt and we sat there, hanging out, eating our breakfast, very chill. I finally got her to tell me the meaning of her name. Her parents named her for her blood type, which is AB positive. Type AB. TAB.

"Is that one of those really rare types?" I asked.

"Yeah," she said. "Only three per cent of people have it."

That didn't surprise me. Everything about Tab was rare. Especially the fact that she liked hanging out with me.

The orange juice carton was covered in condensation. I ran my finger through the moisture, drawing a figure eight over and over.

"Still counting?" Tab asked.

My finger stopped moving.

"Relax," she said. "I saw your lips moving. Dead giveaway."

I looked down at the table, a bit embarrassed. At least she hadn't caught me pulling out my eyebrow hairs.

"Do you count all the time?" Tab asked.

"Pretty much," I said.

"What do you count?"

"Hours. Minutes. Seconds."

"Seconds until what?"

"Until I go home. Until school . . . Until I won't be able to *see* much of anything."

Just saying the word made me depressed. It felt like something was caught in my throat. I pushed the bowl away and looked out the window.

"What's wrong?" said Tab.

I sighed. "It's great we get to stay here this week," I said. "But it's still going to end. Everything's going to end."

Tab found my hand with hers. She traced her finger across my knuckles.

"Will you be coming back next summer?" she asked.

"Depends on my mom's job," I said. "But probably, yeah."

"And how many seconds are in a year?" she asked.

"Thirty-one million. Give or take."

The thought made me so sad I wanted to sink down into the ground and never come back up for air.

"That's not so long to wait," Tab said.

I tried to look in her eyes. Everything was blurrier than normal.

"You have to be careful, though," she said. "If you're so busy counting all those seconds, you'll never notice what's *in* the seconds."

I took a deep breath and stared at our little pile of hands. I wished I could hold this moment hostage for a while.

"I know you're worried about school," she said. "But things are never as bad as we expect. And even if they are, well, you've got friends who can help. You'll have Cheese with you. And I'm just a text message away."

"I guess," I said. "But I hate being scared. I'm scared all the time. I never used to be."

"What are you scared of?"

"Stupid stuff. Crossing busy streets, getting lost downtown, failing school. The list is pretty long actually."

Tab nodded, and she didn't try to tell me not to worry, which was awesome. I hate it when people tell me not to worry.

"Don't be afraid to ask people for help," she said finally.

"I'm not afraid," I said. "I just don't like looking weak."

"Bad vision isn't a weakness," Tab said.

That's nice to say. But we both know it isn't true.

"She's right," said Cheese, suddenly materializing in the doorway.

"Oh, really?" I said. "And how would you know?"

"Easy," said Cheese. "If blindness was a weakness, then how come so many comic book superheroes can't see?"

He walked over to the counter and opened a cupboard. He was wearing his yellow SpongeBob pyjamas. "Think about it," he said. "There's Daredevil, Doctor Mid-Nite, Blindfold, Madame Web . . . Uh, you guys can help me out here if you want."

"Mole Man," I suggested.

"He's a supervillain, but I'll let it slide."

"Cyclops, from *X-Men*," said Tab.

"Nice one."

Cheese rooted around in the cutlery drawer and then came back to the island. He set down a bowl and a spoon and plunked himself down beside Tab. She was still holding my hand. She didn't let go.

"Anyway," said Cheese. "Do you know what those characters have in common? They're all *visionaries*, Finn. They see stuff other people can't. They're all telepathic or clairvoyant or meta-mortal or something."

He still hadn't noticed our hands. "You're talking about *comic books*, Cheese," I said.

"Not just comic books. Ever heard of Tiresias, from Greek mythology? He was the greatest prophet of all. And he was blind."

"I'm not a prophet," I said.

"I agree," said Tab. "You're definitely not."

"I'm not saying you're a prophet," said Cheese. "Only, your

vision problem shouldn't define you. You've got other gifts."

Tab turned to face me. "Is that true? You have gifts?"

"I'm a surprisingly good whistler," I said. "Plus, dogs really like me. And I believe you've experienced my magic?"

Tab squeezed my hand and I remembered what Constant had told me. *Vision is just one way of seeing things. There are plenty of others. Pay attention.*

"You have something better than all that," said Cheese.

"What's better than whistling?" I asked.

"It's obvious," said Cheese. "You've got friends. You've got us."

Tab banged the island with her free hand. "Hear, hear," she said.

My finger stopped tracing that figure-eight pattern on the juice carton. I looked up at Cheese and saw the flash of purple headband, and it made me smile. I thought to myself, *Oh, Cheese, you're one of a kind.*

Cheese tipped some cereal into his bowl. When he reached for the milk, he noticed our hands.

"About time you guys got around to that," he said.

AUTHOR'S NOTE

Writers don't create. They merely pay attention and jot things down. So I'd like to thank the people who did the real work — i.e. who inspired the story, cheered me on as I scribbled and helped mop up my spectacular messes.

First and foremost, my editor Sandy Bogart Johnston. SBJ stands for Supremely Brilliant Juggler, which is totally appropriate, since she effortlessly juggles millions of nouns and verbs and adjectives, and does it while holding my hand, and reminding me to breathe.

Likewise, thanks to Diane Kerner at Scholastic Canada, for reading all the early versions of this book and tactfully pointing out the island-sized holes. Diane, you are my A E I O U and sometimes Y.

A great writer once advised, *If you want to be an author, make interesting friends.* I'm lucky for two friends in particular.

Firstly, Kai Black. Kai is a marathoner, a father and, in spite of being legally blind, an all-round visionary. Kai hit the gas pedal when my life had stalled and taught me that the word *impossible* doesn't exist. This book is for him.

Then there's Rhonda-Marie Avery. Rhonda-Marie runs ultra-marathons the way the rest of us order pizzas. She's also legally blind and works tirelessly to raise awareness of the world's many "other-abled" athletes. In 2015, she founded the Envisions Project — an organization that helps disabled athletes achieve their goals. If not for Rhonda-Marie's wit, wisdom and courage, this book would have no heart, soul or guts.

Thanks also to:

Dr. Lois Calder, O.D., for providing clarity on Stargardt disease. Ben Aylsworth, for helping me nail down the mountain bike sections. Andrea Casault for the great cover. Stella Partheniou Grasso and Kyla Dewar, who made the seconds add up. The extraordinary Bobowski family of Johnstown, New York. My running friends at Blessed Sacrament Catholic School, London. My second family at Brownridge Public School, Vaughan. The warm and generous students of Assiniboia Park Elementary School (Hello, Weyburn!). Talia Schlanger and Kelly Galbraith, for being hope merchants. My brilliant photographer brother, Andy. And, of course, Mom and Dad (as always)!

Other people who picked me up on the trail: Nathan D., Emma Z., Kara, Caelan, Quinn, Kiernan, Sydney, Grace W., Ollie, Jackson, Aaron, Grace S., Benjamin, Mateos, Leonardo, Rowan and Daniel. Mike and Tara. Susan Bedard. Suzanne Brandreth at the Cooke Agency. Julianna Wojcik and Scott Waxman.

Most importantly, thank you Shawna Watson. You are my floating island, my Glimmer Line.

ABOUT THE AUTHOR

David Carroll is the author of *Ultra*, which won two readers' choice awards, a Cybils Award for middle-grade fiction, and was a finalist for a Ruth and Sylvia Schwartz Children's Book Award. David is also a long-distance runner, and a writer and producer for CBC Radio. He lives in Toronto.